THE OMEGA'S PRIZE

TIMBERWOLF LODGE
BOOK 3

VIVIAN AREND

This is a work of fiction. Names, characters, places, and incidents either are the product of the author's imagination or are used fictitiously, and any resemblance to any persons, living or dead, business establishments, events, or locales is entirely coincidental.

The Omega's Prize
Copyright © 2023 by Arend Publishing Inc.
ISBN ebook: 978-1-990674-73-0
ISBN print: 978-1-990674-74-7
Edited by Angie Ramey
Cover Design © Croco Designs
Proofed by: Linda Levy

PRAISE FOR VIVIAN AREND

"Vivian Arend does a wonderful job of building the atmosphere and the other characters in this story so that readers will be sucked into the world and looking forward to the rest of the books in the series."
~ *Library Journal*

"Steamy and sweet complete with a whole host of colourful side characters and enough sub-plots to get your teeth into. A fab read!"
~ *Scorching Book Reviews*

"There's a real chemistry between the characters, laced with humor and snappy dialogue and no shortage of steamy sex scenes to keep things lively. The result is an entertaining, spicy romance."
~ *Publishers Weekly*

I have honestly waited AGES for Vivian to return to her world of shifters and this new trilogy is just what the Romance Witch doctor ordered! The setting is beautiful, the characters are hilarious, and the best friends-to-lovers story never gets old...
~ *Romance Witch Reviews*

Arend offers constant action and thrills, and her characters are so captivating and nuanced that readers will have a hard time guessing who the villains really are.
~ *RT Book Reviews*

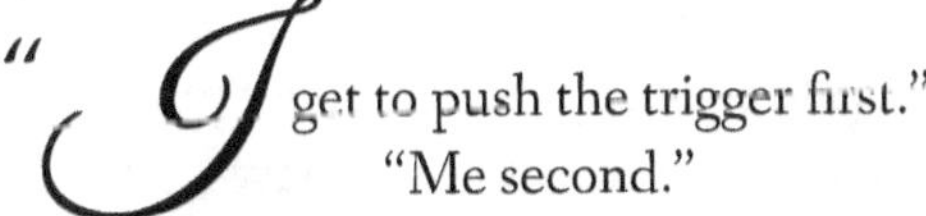

1

———

"I get to push the trigger first."

"Me second."

"I'm bigger than you. I get to do it."

The excited buzz of voices from Stephanie Nix's three nephews danced on the late September air as she sauntered past them. They waved briefly before returning to cajoling their babysitter-slash-teacher-slash-moose-shifter bodyguard, Marvin. Two small bodies, one medium, and one huge.

The four of them sat on the lawn beside Timberwolf Lake, something shiny in the middle of their huddle. Curiosity hit Stephanie for an instant then slid off. As much fun as it was sharing adventures with the kiddos, she was on a different mission. The good weather had enticed her to start her day with a walk around the lake, but it was time to get to work.

Sort of. What was work, anyway? If she truly enjoyed what she was doing, could she ever complain about her daily tasks? She thought not.

It had been a good night, following hard on the heels of a great weekend and a fantastic summer...

No, she needed a better word. A very *unforgettable* summer.

Finding out the remote wilderness lodge she, her sister, and her bestie had won in a lottery included a werewolf pack—not a typical agenda item. So far, so good, though.

Stephanie whistled happily as she bounced up the back porch steps two at a time. She slipped off her shoes at the door then hopped into the kitchen and twirled her sister, Stacy, into a quick, vigorous hug. "You're making me tuna casserole for supper."

"I think I'm making it for everyone," Stacy teased. She tugged her ponytail a little tighter, her brown eyes flashing with amusement. "But yes, you might get to have some. *If* you've gotten your chores done."

Stephanie folded her arms over her chest and glared. "Look, *Wolf Mom*, just because the pack has embraced your matronly ways with open arms, that doesn't mean you're the boss of me." She dipped her chin firmly.

Her sister raised a brow. "What? No, *so there?* No sticking out your tongue?"

"I'm embracing my inner adult."

A sharp snort escaped Stacy. "Good luck with that." She snapped the dish towel in her hands at Stephanie's butt. "Out of my kitchen, varmint. Or I'll make you wash dishes."

"Wouldn't, couldn't, shouldn't." But Stephanie danced out of range as quickly as possible. Stacy was an evil mastermind when it came to towel marksmanship.

One quick dash put Stephanie around the corner and into the living room. Here, the third member of her gal-pal trio stared at an industrial-size easel covered with fabric

Northern Lights Shifters

Wolf Signs

Wolf Flight

Wolf Games

Wolf Tracks

Wolf Line

Wolf Nip

Copper King

Laird Wolf

Black Gold

Silver Mine

Diamond Dust

Moon Shine

A Lady's Heart

Wild Prince

Borealis Bears

The Bear's Chosen Mate

The Bear's Fated Mate

The Bear's Forever Mate

A full list of Vivian's print titles is available on her website

www.vivianarend.com

swatches, magazine clippings of clothing and food, and an outrageous number of Post-it notes.

"Collaging without me?" Stephanie pretended to be outraged. "Hand over the glue stick now, and no one will get hurt."

Cassidy shook her head, her dark brown hair bouncing lightly as she gestured her friend forward. "I'm good at some parts of this job, but not so good at others. I'm trying to conjure up wild inspiration."

"What exactly are we being inspired to do?"

Her bestie wrinkled her nose as she moved a sticky note that said *family event* from the square labeled *December* to the one labeled *March*. "Master planning themes and events for the coming year. We had a successful soft opening last week, but we only have nine months to get final approval from the powers that be. I want to make sure Timberwolf Lodge is ours for good."

"It's going well so far, though, right?" Stephanie eyed the collage closer. "And last week was not a success; it was a *screaming* success. Everyone who attended said that if they had a say in the matter, we'd already have won the challenge."

The impossible, incredible challenge.

When Cassidy had tossed their names into the hat the previous spring and won Timberwolf Lodge in a lottery, there had been one caveat. They had to prove themselves to the *Wilson Pack* to make the win official and final. After the past three months, that nebulous phrase had become clear to mean they had to impress a bunch of werewolves.

No prob. Maybe.

Stephanie eyed the chart again. "I suggest you switch to making to-do lists and adding less pictures. Because right now, I'm worried you're planning a Valentine's Day massacre or a black wedding."

Cassidy blinked then leaned toward the easel, adjusting pictures. "Oops. My Post-its slipped."

"Good to know. Because enormous, black-handled knives stabbing into flowers might become a trend, but more likely, *not...*"

"Hey, you never know. Look how axe throwing took off."

"Axe throwing is a useful and daily activity in many households." Stephanie kept a straight face as she said it.

Her bestie did not disappoint. Cass tilted her head and gave her *the look*. "Daily?"

"Of course." Steph smiled sweetly. "That is what you and Jace are doing in your cabin every night, yes? To cause the constant loud thumping noises?"

Cassidy's cheeks flared to red. Her mouth opened and closed a couple times, then she narrowed her eyes. "You're eavesdropping."

"I have very sensitive hearing. Or you're very loud. Possibly both." Stephanie flitted backward out of swinging range. "I can stay and help if you want."

"Nah. Not right now. I've already got your list of spa-specific ideas. Once I figure out how to balance it all and we're getting to the details stage, you can absolutely break out your list-making skills and we'll have a blast planning minutia."

"Right up my alley. Now, I should go annoy my favourite wolf."

"Say hi to Blue for me," Cassidy offered as she turned back to her task, focus already off Stephanie.

Maybe she should have felt guilty. Both her chicas were hard at work, yet here she was, lazing as she walked out the massive oversized front door of the Timberwolf Lodge into the refreshing fall air. Her shoes were on the other side of the house, so she paced forward silently in her socks.

Nope. Guilt was not allowed. She worked hard as well, just not right this instant. Running a spa in the lodge meant she'd worked non-stop while they'd had guests. She also put in long hours helping with the rest of the lodge tasks.

If she wanted to take a breather and go sit with Blue Carter for a while, she was allowed. Her meditations that morning had emphasized the need to take some *me* time over the coming days, so she would. She liked to listen to the universe and go along with its guidance. Life usually worked out better that way.

Stephanie stopped two steps onto the porch and eyed the man. Long, lean, yet muscular. A mop of surfer-blond hair that was piled up on his head today in a man bun.

Blue Carter was...unique.

In a pack of strong individuals, he sat outside of the norm in just about every category.

Cassidy's mate, Jace, was powerful and a capital A-Alpha. Borderline asshole at moments, but then again, so was Cassidy. They were like a matched set of bossy bookends.

Stacy's mate was Delaney, and he was the Enforcer for the pack. It seemed to mean a whole lot more handholding and encouraging talks than ripping out throats, which went well with her sister's style of parenting. Stacy was all tough love yet big heart, always willing and ready to listen to her three boys, and now, to all the teens in the pack who'd started hanging around in droves.

Blue was the pack Omega. Not the boss, not the parent. Mostly he acted like a court jester, but Stephanie thought some of that was for show. She found him charming and easy to be around. He wore brightly coloured clothing, gaudy to the extreme, in a way that said he was trying to be annoying. His heart was kind, yet he had more than enough *oomph* so that no one pushed him around.

Although that might have been the mystical Omega *woo-woo* stuff that the other wolves in their lives tried to explain but mostly couldn't. 'Blue knows things,' they said. 'Blue settles people down,' they said.

Stephanie eyed him a little longer. Whatever *they* said, Blue had proven to be a good friend over the past three months. She liked having more friends in her life.

When she was still a few steps away from the porch swing, Blue closed his eyes and made the most pathetic sound. "Not what I want to listen to," he complained.

"You have an ear bud in the other ear?" The swing rocked as she joined him. "Because I don't hear anything."

Blue's eyes snapped open, and he jerked upright in shock. "How did you sneak up on me like that?" he grumbled.

She lifted a hand in front of his face and shimmied her fingers. "Maybe I'm magic."

MAYBE SHE WAS.

As far as Blue and his wolf were concerned, Stephanie was the be-all and end-all of his dreams. His fated mate. Eventually.

Which was a weird comment for a wolf, even an Omega wolf.

He'd known since the first day the ladies arrived at Timberwolf Lodge that she was the one for him...but not yet.

He knew that made no sense at all. Fated mates were *fated* mates, only the connection between him and Steph was more like having all the ingredients for a cake sitting on the table. No one would call it a cake until they put everything together in the right order and baked it for long enough.

Which meant he was stuck continuing as he had over the past months. He kept his need for her in check and controlled the urge he had to claim her, even as they bantered lightly.

He snorted, then eyed her closer. "Stocking feet on the porch? You're going to catch a cold, young lady."

Stephanie wiggled closer then threw a blanket over both their legs. "Sitting in the cold without a jacket? You're going to catch pneumonia, or as Ace would say, pee-uwww-moan-ya."

Heaven and hell. Blue planned to apply for sainthood ASAP, because he lifted his arm, curled it around her shoulders, and tucked her into his side. Friendly-like. Just good ol' pals. Buddies with his fated mate.

Sainthood was definitely up for grabs since he wasn't tucking her under him and taking a big, giant bite. "We'll both catch the sniffles. Stacy will make us chicken soup, and Cassidy will make us watch creepy old movies where everyone makes bad choices, to be sure we keep our spirits high."

"I heard that," Cassidy called through the window behind them.

"Eavesdropping from the living room again. You're so needy," Stephanie sang out, shouting at her best friend.

"I'm right here. And you're talking about me," Cassidy complained.

"So don't be right there. Isn't Jace home? Go find your

wolf. Throw axes with him or something." Stacy twisted away from the lodge and took a deep, happy breath. "That is one hell of a view."

"The snowline is sticking around." Blue pointed to the very tip where the faintest brush of white covered the peaks.

Beside him, Steph shivered. "Chilly. It's so exciting. Our first winter at Timberwolf Lodge."

"Successful first visitors this past week was also exciting. Everyone seemed pleased."

"So, *so* much fun when it was our own lodge and my own studio," Stephanie agreed, then she shrugged. "Not a perfect homerun, though. I need to schedule my time better and see if there's anyone in town who can help if things get extra busy. I hated to turn people away, but I was booked solid."

"You were too busy," Blue complained. "I barely saw you for nearly a week."

"Aww, did you miss me?"

"I did," he admitted readily.

Stephanie hummed softly. "Well, I sort of missed you, too. But you were also busy. With Jace refusing to leave Cassidy's side, and Del claiming he was needed at the Lodge as well, someone had to make sure everyone else in the pack behaved."

"Yeah, I was swamped. Very busy having multiple cups of coffee, tea, and way too much cake. Everyone in this pack makes cake, and I love pie more," he shared.

His cake and mates analogy might have something to do with that.

"I'll remember that," Steph promised.

Thank goodness his Omega skills weren't completely messed up. Just the one where he usually knew things a little before they happened. As if the future was a whole lot blurrier now than before.

He had his suspicions it had something to do with Stephanie being his mate. They weren't there yet...but maybe it was getting closer. Not that he could tell for certain right now.

Fah.

Or maybe it was because of Emma Wilson. An evil, grasping-for-power wolf who had been cast out of the pack a couple of weeks ago by their Enforcers. Blue had a gut feeling that Timberwolf Lodge hadn't heard the last of her.

Stephanie rested her head on his shoulder, and for a split second, something sizzled up Blue's skin to the back of his neck. It was gone before he could analyze it.

Not an electric shock. Steph didn't seem to notice. So he tilted his head enough that they connected gently, touching each other from hip to head as they stared at the mountains.

Connected...but not yet.

His wolf tended to like to ramble, so the fact the four words were all he said before falling silent seemed odd. Blue knew well enough not to fight for more information.

It would happen when it was supposed to. *They* would happen. He was sure of it.

Dear God, just don't make him wait too much longer or he was going to turn into a bundle of furry frustration. Not a good place for an Omega wolf to hang out. He'd end up making the entire pack jittery.

But here and now, Blue took the small bit of affection Stephanie was comfortable giving him and savoured it.

He nudged her lightly with his elbow. "This is nice."

"Yeah," she said, her long, slow breaths matching time with his. "It is."

They grinned at each other. Blue stared into her eyes. Sometimes he thought he should win a prize for being patient beyond belief. Then she'd look at him with those big, bright-blue eyes, and he knew he'd wait forever if that's what it took.

"It's so nice and peaceful." She winked. "Means something is bound to come along any second now and blow it all up."

"Oh, you bright and shining optimist."

"Ain't I just?" she agreed.

That's when the explosion happened.

An enormous *boom* echoed off the buildings and distant mountains, ringing in their ears as amusement vanished and they both shot to their feet.

A billowing cloud of smoke rose over the roof of Timberwolf Lodge.

2

———

She couldn't run as fast as Blue, but she had a sneaky suspicion she knew where to aim him. "Lakeside. Marvin was with the kids."

Blue zoomed ahead of her, feet moving like a blur. He vanished before she'd finished speaking.

By the time she rounded the second corner of the lodge, the smoke had mostly cleared from ground level. A burn mark on the grass showed where the explosion had taken place, but while there were four bodies on the ground feet away from the scorch mark, the boys all seemed to be shrieking with laughter, not pain.

"That was so cool."

Blaze's shout of delight was followed by a *woohoo* and a *wheeee* as all three boys, Colt, Blaze, and Ace, bounced upright. The kids pulled ear protection off their heads and held them to their chests as they raced toward where Blue was helping Marvin to his feet.

"Wow. That was...unexpected." The massive man who was nanny and teacher to the children of Timberwolf Lodge loomed above six-foot-tall Blue. Marvin's tangled beard and mane of hair were messier than normal, and that was saying something.

"You didn't know you were about to blow something up?" Stacy had arrived from the direction of the kitchen. Her quick, knowledgeable glance over her boys spotted no injuries, which seemed to settle her anger.

"Oh, the goal was to blow it up," Marvin admitted.

"It was a rocket ship, Mama," Ace told her excitedly, pointing across the lake to where a shiny silver triangle floated lazily toward the water line, the parachute above it sweeping gently left then right.

"Only, I don't think there should be that much smoke." Colt held the instructions in front of him. He twisted them closer, then away, frowning as he read.

Blaze bounced on the spot, his grin widening. Stephanie knew it for the classic *I have a joke I need to tell*. Either that or he had to pee. "Blaze, what's on your mind?"

Vibrating with happiness, he turned to her. "Know what steps a wolf takes when he sees an explosion?"

"No, what steps?" she asked obediently like the awesome auntie she was.

"Big ones!"

Snickering sounded from the gathered group which now included Jace and Cassidy. The boys' new father figure, Del, was the only pack leadership missing as he had appointments that morning in town at his law office.

Marvin's expression went sheepish as he glanced around at the gathering. "Didn't mean for that to happen. Believe me, the boys were all a good distance away. Safety gear in place and all that."

Stephanie laid a reassuring hand on his arm. "Of course, they were.

The twisting of the moose shifter's facial features was

made odder than expected by the fact *Marvin* had clearly not been well out of reach of the disaster. How should she tell him?

Blue took the lead and cleared his throat. "Um, Marvin?"

"Yeah?" The big man waved a hand in the air, wafting the lingering smoke away, not realizing he was the source.

"You're missing something." Blue kept his expression blank, pointing to his own eyebrows. "Mostly gone."

Marvin pursed his lips, which with the missing brows made him look rather comical. He touched his face gingerly, then shrugged. "Well. That's something I've never tried before."

"Come on, kids. Let's introduce Marvin to the wonderful world of antiseptic cream and possibly a bit of brow liner." Stacy caught her son by the hand before Ace could race off to retrieve the cap of the rocket. "And you are on chef's helper duty."

"But Mama, the rocket—"

"I'll get it," Jace promised. "Your mama needs your help, or we won't have lunch on time."

Ace's eyes widened. "Okay."

He trotted off with his brothers and mom, guiding a still slightly dazed Marvin to the kitchen.

Cassidy poked her toe into the burn spot. "I suppose it was worth it. In the name of science and all that."

"There's extra grass seed in the garden shed. I can deal with this," Blue promised.

"Thanks." Cass caught Jace's fingers in hers. "I'll walk with you to retrieve the rocket ship parts. I need a brain break."

Which left Stephanie standing beside Blue on scorched earth. He bent to stroke his fingers over the blackened space. She leaned over and sniffed. "Ugh. Can you really fix it?"

"Sure. Not really me, but time. Plus a lot of grass seed." He grinned at her. "So much for our cozy, relaxing cuddle on the porch."

"Adrenaline is good for the system, or so I've been told." She focused on the reason she'd sought him out in the first place. "I was wondering if I could get your help today. After you're done being garden guru."

"Of course. I'm all yours."

Too easy. She eyed him. "You know, I ask you for a lot of favours. You always say yes without first asking what I need help with."

Blue shrugged. "Doesn't really matter. If you need help, you need help. Who am I to say, 'Gee, you want help with that thing I don't like to do? Nah, you're on your own.' That would be a shitty way to act as a friend."

"Maybe. But still, that doesn't mean that's not what some people do."

"I'm not some people." Blue winked. "What are we doing?"

"Testing my new acupuncture needles. I'm not sure, but they might have sent ones that are too long."

His expression didn't change. Much. A small flutter of his eyelashes and a twitch at his hairline were the only tells. "Oh. Okay."

Stephanie fought her grin. Not that she *wanted* to scare him...

Yes, yes she did. Easygoing or not, Blue needed to learn this lesson. "I'm pretty sure I remember all the placement rules, but I should refresh my memory for the groin area and the base of the feet. Probably a dozen needles in each spot, and we'll be golden."

Blue swallowed visibly but kept a sort of smile in place. "Um. Clarifying. You want to put needles in my groin and in the soles of my feet?"

"Yup." She caught him by the elbow and marched him toward the lodge, mostly so he couldn't see her face because she was one step away from losing it.

He walked with her for about three steps before jerking to a complete and utter stop. "Wait."

Thank. God.

Still, she had to play this one out to the end. She blinked innocently. "Yes?"

Blue narrowed his gaze. "*You.*"

"Me?"

"You're pulling my leg."

"Why would I do that?"

He hesitated. "To teach me a lesson?"

"Whyever would you need lessons, Blue? Or should I call you Mr. Cooperative?"

With a gentle snort, he twisted to face her then offered another smile. A genuine one this time. "Steph, what do you really need help with?"

"I got a shipment of massage oils. I need to test them both for scent and basically slickness, so I'm good on what to use where. Can I give you a massage tonight?"

"Oh. Well, I don't know if I should help with that. Sounds like a slippery slope. First you're going to want to give me a massage, and the next thing I know, you're putting me in an ice-filled tub and harvesting my kidneys."

Amusement made her snort in a most unladylike way. "Good job. That's a leap from, 'Of course, I'm all yours.'"

He grinned. "Just making sure *you* were paying attention. Yes, I would love a massage, even if it means I'll end up smelling like a flower bouquet exploded. After supper? Before?"

"After, please. I have a bunch of other things to deal with first."

"Then I am your willing victim. Later."

Impulsively, she hugged him. "You're the best."

"I am." He patted her back and stepped out of her embrace. He winked then turned, whistling softly as he headed to the garden shed.

Good man. Good friend.

A soft bubble of happiness burst inside, tingling upward from her belly toward her heart. Coming to Timberwolf Lodge had been such a good move.

Especially since it got me farther away from things better not remembered.

BLUE WAITED until he was all the way inside the garden shed before collapsing against the wall and groaning like a zombie. "*Whyyyyyyy.* Why must she torment me like this?"

Yet he knew damn well that after dinner he'd march his ass up to Steph's spa room and allow her to put her hands all over him.

Masochist. He must have previously unbeknownst-to-him masochistic leanings.

Suck it up, sweetheart. Someday, our ship will arrive.

Landlocked. Just saying.

Blue pulled himself together then dug around until he found the grass seed and some potting soil.

He also found a bit of youthful memorabilia that made him grin and offered an idea for a lovely afternoon distraction. Tonight, he would suffer. But after his work was done, here was mischief they all could enjoy.

Prepping the burn spot and reseeding took about an hour, after which he returned to the shed for his treasures.

He hauled the disc golf baskets and the gym bag full of discs onto an unburnt section of lawn closer to the trees. There were only nine baskets, but that was more than enough to start with. He eyed the terrain and mentally considered the possible flight paths for different shots.

Del showed up just as Blue placed the third basket into position. "Seriously? I haven't played in years."

"Last time I remember Uncle J had these up was nearly fifteen years ago." Blue nodded his thanks as Del helped level the goal used for the game. A flattish wire basket circled a vertical pole at about hip height, with a metal circle a couple feet higher. The top circle held a series of chains that hung into a U shape in the middle that they'd try to hit with the frisbees. "I think Auntie Rachel told him to take them down because there was a garden party planned along with some bigwig wedding, and she didn't want random discs flying everywhere into wedding cakes and punch bowls."

"Gee, I wonder how she got the idea that disc golf was a dangerous sport." Del stepped back, grabbed a disc, and spun it at the basket. It slipped out of his hand, bounced off the chain, and rebounded into Blue's gut. He coughed even as Del swore. "Sorry. Out of practice."

Blue pressed a hand to his belly, laughing around the lack of air. "I don't know. You used to hit me all the time back then, too."

Del snorted but then admitted, "Sometimes."

"Why do you think I started dressing the way I do?" Blue demanded. "It was the only way to stop you guys from being all, 'Oh, gee. Sorry, Blue. Didn't see you standing there in the middle of the empty lawn. My bad.'"

"You were a good target," Del admitted.

"I'm supposed to be the pack Omega. Don't know how you managed to abuse me so."

Del was outright laughing now. "Poor little Omega."

"I was treated terribly. Still am to this day."

"I can see that. You usually deserve it."

They grinned at each other. Only the closest of family could understand Blue's complaint to be a boast.

Omegas were unique. Special even, and there was a time when Blue had been treated *too* nicely by the pack. No one wanted to upset him or hurt him, even by accident. Which made sense but didn't.

Try explaining to a ten-year-old why no one wants you on their baseball team.

When Jace and Del had decided to treat Blue like one of the guys, it had been the start of the best days in his life. Shoved during tag? Muddy and wet from wrestling in the forest? Bruised from falling out of the treehouse? Okay, that one had been mostly his own fault.

Still, being treated like he was ordinary was the best thing ever.

Which meant it was time to put all the ghosts of the past years to rest. Blue wasn't sure why, but as they paced toward the first tee box to start a round of disc golf, it seemed important.

"I've gotten over you being a jerk. You know, when you kicked Jace out and spent those years being Alpha, you were an ass. But I forgive you." Blue shared it as if announcing the sky was blue.

"So big of you." Del raised a brow. "Did I sound concerned that you don't like me, or something?"

"I know you've been crying into your pillow over it for weeks." Blue patted him on the shoulder. "It's time to let it go."

"Start singing, and I'll throw you instead of the disc."

Oh, so tempting. But more than the urge to make mischief, Blue was compelled to speak again. "Serious for a moment. You did okay. It wasn't where Jasper pack should have been, but that wasn't your fault. You did the best you could, and now it's time to move to the next stage. Jace and Cassidy. You and Stacy."

All teasing pushed aside, Del paused, his arms folded over his chest as he met Blue's gaze evenly. They stayed that way for a moment, and then Del dipped his chin. When he spoke, there was nothing lighthearted in his tone, but it held complete acceptance and respect. "I hear you, Omega of the Jasper pack. Thanks for what you did to keep the pack together until we found this new path forward."

A knot Blue hadn't realized existed unfurled in his core. It was as if he'd been clenching his stomach muscles, and now he could relax and breath freely.

He shook his head lightly. "Okay, that was weird."

"Trust me, Blue. Conversations with you are rarely simple." But Del offered him a hand then pulled him in for a hug and firm back pounding. When they separated, Del raised a brow. "Did you know when you slip into uber-Omega mode these days, you glow?"

Blue blinked. "Really?"

"No." Del grinned. "Just fucking with you."

It couldn't be helped. Blue tackled his friend to the ground and they wrestled like teenagers. Which was where they still were when two pairs of boots stopped beside them.

"I'm pretty sure they're not actually trying to kill each other." Stacy's solid alto stopped them cold.

"There would probably be less growling and laughing involved in actual bloodshed," Stephanie agreed. She rested her hands on her knees and leaned down, meeting Blue's gaze evenly. "I spotted the baskets from out my window. Don't even try to deny it. If you hand over the discs, nobody will get hurt."

He held his hand out to her, just to torment himself a little as she helped him up. Stacy had done the same for Del, but he did a neat little trick at the end that finished with her in his arms and the two of them lip locked.

Stephanie sighed. "You two do that far too often."

Her sister pulled back, still staring into Del's eyes. "We're still newlyweds."

Stephanie turned to Blue and made a face, sticking out her tongue and pretending to gag. Blue shrugged. Not much more he wanted to do than to pull Stephanie into his arms and plant one on her.

Not yet, his wolf warned. *Not yet but... Soon?*

The unexpected announcement meant Blue was still blinking when Stephanie shoved a disc into his hand. "Okay, kissy-poos. We're partnering up. Blue and I challenge you to a duel."

3

———

As far as wild, rambunctious activities went, this was low on the scary scale. Still, as Stephanie and Blue took turns flinging their discs toward the basket, amusement and laughter rose rapidly.

Del had a wicked forehand, which meant with the slight flick of his wrist he managed to send his discs swirling around impossible corners. Stephanie had some tricks of her own, though.

Blue's jaw dropped in astonishment as she stepped up and threw a disc with her left hand. It spun prettily past the tangle of rosebushes that would've otherwise barred the way. "How did you do that?"

She grabbed him by the hand and pulled him toward where the disc now sat an easy putt away from the basket. "Ambidextrous."

"Get out. I did not know that."

She shrugged. "I can't do everything with both hands. I mostly write with my right hand, but there's a lot of stuff that I use my left for instead."

They played the first half of the baskets Blue had put

into place, Stephanie happily pacing by his side. "It's too bad we didn't get these up for the entire summer," she said.

"I had no idea they were still here," he shared. "We used to have enough for a full eighteen hole course. The rest of them must be in a storage shed somewhere else on the property."

"Nine will be fine for now." She tilted her head and raised her voice toward her sister. "We can kick their butts just fine with nine holes."

"You need to stop cheating," Stacy called back.

Stephanie twirled toward her, pressed a hand to her chest, and slipped on her best outraged expression. "Moi? Cheat? *Never.*"

It was the honest truth. It seemed the skills she'd acquired many years ago hadn't faded. And when it came to the final hole and Blue missed his putt, Stephanie marched up to the spot and confidently threw her disc in without taking any time at all.

Del eyed her with curiosity as he shook her hand and offered congratulations. "That's quite the arm you got on you."

Stephanie smiled broadly. "Ultimate Frisbee. Five years during college."

Her sister narrowed her gaze for a moment. "Seriously? I didn't think the sports were related."

"Lots of skills that have overlap," Blue said with an approving nod. He slipped his arm around Stephanie's shoulders in a side hug. "My partner is the best."

"Thank you. You're pretty cool, too," Stephanie offered, anchoring him to her with a hand around his waist.

Something cool and refreshing wafted over her in the second that he met her gaze and winked. Her heart pounded a couple of times, and her throat tightened a little. It was—

Then they were surrounded by a mass of kids, their nanny, and the rest of the Timberwolf Lodge staff who had all come out to check out the latest activity.

Stacy clapped and held her hands in the air. "I have chili planned for supper. There's no reason why we can't move that into an outdoor meal if everybody wants to play some more disc golf and have a bonfire tonight."

Five-year-old Ace came up and tugged his mom's hand. "Dixie and Miss Sophie can come to supper too, yes?"

Stacy tapped her youngest on the nose with a fingertip. "Yes." She glanced around at everybody gathered around them. "How does that sound?"

A chorus of cheers went up, and the group tugged into different directions. Blue and Del were swamped by the boys wanting to learn how to play this new game. Jace marched in another direction with Marvin, while Cassidy headed back to the Lodge with Stacy.

Stephanie stood at the edge of the forest and watched as everybody eagerly moved to the next thing.

Her feet stayed planted on the spot. Her heart still raced as if something extraordinary had just happened.

Blue had just happened.

Stephanie pressed a hand to the space between her throat and her chest and felt the pounding rhythm of the blood pumping through her. She took a deep breath, and the scent of him—snowcapped mountains and cool running river—filled her head even though he was now twenty feet away, Blaze riding his back as if Blue were a pony.

Stephanie was old enough to have figured out some things in life. She'd never been boy crazy, or girl crazy, as a teen. She'd listened to her friends ramble on about their crushes, and there'd been a while when she pretended to really like so-and-so. Mostly to keep everybody from discovering a secret.

But to her, *like* had the same connection as liking a pretty painting or staring out at a pristine landscape. It was something out there to enjoy, not something she wanted for herself. As if watching another a person enjoy a fantastic meal but never being tempted to take a bite.

The first time she'd been tempted to *take a bite* had been with her good friend in high school. Tim and she had been on the drama team, and while prepping for the big annual yearly production they'd spent a lot of time together. Time together that had eventually moved from building a bedroom scene to checking out the bedsprings.

And yes, this was partly about sex, but also about connection. Sex was only one part of it. Stephanie twisted on the spot and eyed Blue again. She imagined standing next to him or cuddling up like they had been on the porch. Comfortable. Friends who knew a lot about each other and cared about each other. Connected—

Oh. My. God.

Her phone rang, and she fumbled for it, hitting *Accept* while her brain whirled with the possibilities and questions of her realization. "Hey, Angie. What's shaking?"

"Got a call from one of the suppliers we've been trying to get a hold of for a while. He's headed out on a walkabout and wanted to know when someone can come to pick up the artwork he's been doing. He asked for you specifically. François somebody?"

"Fantastic. Of course we can come get them." She concentrated, turning her back on the guys so she wouldn't be distracted by her previous mental loops. "We can take a truck into Jasper first thing in the morning."

"He doesn't have the work in the art store in Jasper," Angie warned. "He said he'll leave it all in the cabin and studio, so you'll have to come and get it."

Now there was a twist. "But he lives up the mountain."

On the other end of the line, the older wolf snickered. "There are a few mountains in the area, darlin'. You want to get a little more specific?"

"I would if I could, but I can't," Stephanie recited before sighing heavily. "This is going to be a bigger task than expected. I don't think I can do it on my own. Let me talk to the guys tonight, and we'll come up with a solution."

"Sounds like a plan. And holy crap, girl. I just opened his website. You got a world-famous artist to do paintings for Timberwolf Lodge?"

"I've been following his work for years. I sent an email when I first saw something he'd done, and we've kept in touch since then."

Angie whistled softly. "You have good taste in friends."

"I do, *friend*," Stephanie teased.

The other woman laughed. "Thanks, *friend*. Okay, I'll let him know you got the message and will be in touch."

She hung up, and now thoroughly distracted, Stephanie pushed aside the problem of Blue and considered the new issue. François Andean had been very generous when she contacted him about art for the lodge. Which meant she now had to find a way to get said artwork out of the mountains in one piece.

Another new adventure. Hopefully one that would not end up with anyone broken.

~

SOMEHOW, even though chili was on the menu, Blue still ended up standing beside the barbecue watching Jace expertly handle steaks.

"Because I don't serve you enough protein," Stacy complained, but she smiled, walking past them to place two large bowls of salad on the over-long picnic table Blue had constructed so that they could all eat together.

"Never enough protein," Jace agreed. "Don't worry. They'll be done in just a few minutes."

From her position at the table, Blaze on one side and Ace on the other, Stephanie snickered. "Do you even have the heat turned on? Because most of the time, your steaks are still mooing when they hit the plate."

"He cooks them just fine," Cassidy protested. "Exactly the way I like them. Blue-rare."

Stephanie leaned back and gave her best friend a tormented look. "Which is a thing I have never understood about you. Nearly raw steak, and yet you squirm at the mere thought of sushi."

Cassidy shuddered visibly.

The boys at the table giggled. "Auntie Cassidy, sushi is good," Colt informed her.

She met his eyes steadily. "Sushi is very good—if I were a shark."

They kept bantering, but Jace nudged Blue's shoulder. "Hey. Information you need to know. Del, come tell Blue what you told me earlier."

Del pressed a kiss to Stacy's temple then left her at the table. Casually, he joined Blue and Jace by the barbecue but twisted so he could keep the rest of the family in his line of sight. "Remember that Dwight guy who claimed to be the brother of my wife's ex-husband? Trying to track her down regarding some fictitious inheritance?"

Blue didn't need the reminder. The father to Blaze and Ace had turned out to be a piece of work, and Stacy had divorced him years ago. Still, he was missing and not a person they wanted to reestablish contact with. A mysterious brother was even less welcome. "Lives in the Toronto area. The local pack was keeping an eye on him for us, yes?"

"The local pack sent me an email that sometime between last night and this morning, Dwight vanished."

The hell? "They *lost* him?"

"It's been two months, and in all that time he's kept to a very regulated routine. But somewhere between entering his house last night before six p.m. and this morning, he must have bolted." Jace lowered his voice, making sure that the chatting, laughing group at the table couldn't hear him. "When he didn't come out of the house at seven thirty like usual, someone went and checked the house. It was empty of any personal possessions. Just furniture and dishes remained."

Blue's confusion grew. "How does someone pack up all his possessions and leave without the people watching him knowing what was going on?" Anger flared in his gut. "Did someone in the pack get paid off to let him escape?"

Del shook his head. "That's the first thing I thought of, but I've gotten to know their Alpha over the last while, and he said he questioned everyone personally. None of them did anything they shouldn't have."

This was not good news. Until now, the mysterious Dwight had been a maybe problem. He'd sent an email attempting to find information about Stacy, but low-key enough it could've been just a coincidence.

Him vanishing turned this into a capital letter Big Deal.

Jace pulled the perfectly seared steaks off the grill and

piled them onto a platter. "Not much else we can do now, but we wanted you to know. We'll up security around here, just in case."

"You and Del take care of that. I've got a couple other things to think about. I'll let you know if it'll work." Because he had contacts that might give them another place to start.

Gathering at the table with the rest of them, Blue pushed down his concern and focused on the feeling of family. The feeling of unity.

It wasn't only being here at Timberwolf Lodge. It was the people, and with the final bit of tension gone between him and Del, they truly were his family.

He met Stephanie's gaze across the table and smiled.

She blinked then stumbled in her conversation with her oldest nephew. Even as she listened to what Colt was telling her, she kept glancing over at Blue, and...

Was she blushing?

Inside, his wolf wagged his tail. Just once, which was a good thing because it was a very odd sensation considering Blue was fully human and currently sitting on his butt. But still, something was going on.

Oh, for the ability to *know*. Usually he'd have an inner sense of what was going on, but that had frozen in place when it came to dealing with Stephanie. So Blue did what he usually did when there was nothing else to do; he enjoyed the time with his family. Listened to the happy voices as his pack mates made the bonds between themselves stronger, more intense.

And he waited and watched, because something— nothing specific that he could tell but was still aware enough to know—*something* had begun to change.

They'd made it halfway through desert when Stephanie sat upright. "Shoot. I can't believe I forgot to say something before now. Jace," she turned to face the man, "remember I ordered artwork for the lodge? Angie told me today that it's ready to be picked up."

"Good news. I can't wait to see what he made for us," Cassidy said enthusiastically.

"Me too, but here's the complication. We have to go up to his studio to grab it."

Del whistled. "You got an invite to his studio? That's like a never-happens thing."

Stephanie shrugged. "He's not going to be there, but I take it this isn't the kind of place where I can drive the SUV."

Jace shook his head. "Blue's Jeep is the best bet. That's going to be a heck of a trip, though."

"That's going to be one slow trip coming out unless he hasn't framed anything and they're all still in transport tubes," Blue pointed out.

Stephanie made a face. "The specialty frames are kind of part of the picture."

Blue held his hands in the air. "Can't be helped. When can we go?"

She considered. "Probably sooner than later. I don't have a ton of things happening in the next couple of days."

"You need to be here on Thursday," Del reminded Blue. "We're being invaded by the teens of the pack and having you around will help a lot with all the drama."

Cassidy waved a hand. "We'll just sic Stacy on them."

Stacy wrinkled her nose. "They are a lovely group of young adults with a healthy helping of angst and flaring wolf hormones. So yes, Blue, you do need to be here."

"First thing tomorrow works for me." Blue checked his calendar on his phone to be sure but then nodded as he met Stephanie's gaze. "There're a couple things I need to get done tonight, though. We'll have to move the massage to a later date. I'll be ready to leave at five."

Her jaw swung open. "Okay."

He chuckled. "It's a good two hour drive up to François's property. It might take an additional hour to drive out if we're being uber-careful. And I don't know how much packing we'll have to do at the other end."

"Makes sense."

Across the table, Blaze met Blue's gaze. "Uncle Blue? Do you know when frogs get up?"

He leaned forward across the table. "No. When do they get up?"

"At the croak of dawn," Blaze announced cheerfully.

Stephanie laughed and then ruffled Blaze's hair. "It's nice to see you branching out from the wolf jokes. All comedians need to have a well-rounded repertoire."

"That's what Mom said."

Stephanie met her sister's gaze and winked. "Smart Mom." She turned back to Blue. "Then I guess we're going to make like frogs. I'll be sure to hop right in when you get here."

4

———

It was early enough to have the excuse of being too tired to talk, Stephanie justified. That small bubble of confusing emotion remained balanced between her heart and the back of her throat, leaving her strangely speechless.

Thank goodness there were enough other things to occupy her as Blue turned them off the main highway outside of Jasper onto a narrow but still paved road.

There was something she could talk about safely. "This doesn't seem like too bad of a road."

Blue sat relaxed behind the wheel, one hand resting at two o'clock and the other holding the to-go coffee Stacy had made for them. "Enjoy this, because at some point were going to find out exactly how well your fillings are attached."

Stephanie grinned. "No fillings."

"Get out."

"Stephanie demonstrates excellent oral hygiene." She said it as if quoting an older and more sophisticated person, but then she ruined it by snickering. "Also, one dental hygienist told me that I have extraordinarily hard enamel and unless I went around drilling holes in my own teeth I probably will have no issues, ever."

"Wolves also have excellent oral hygiene, but that's because some of the magic of shifting back and forth seems to take care of ordinary things like gum disease and —" he stopped suddenly. "Are we really talking about teeth and gums?"

"You brought it up," Stephanie protested. "Also, I think it's fascinating. I have so many questions about the whole life-as-a-werewolf thing, but it seems very impersonal to demand a biology 101 class. I like it when you share little tidbits."

Blue's expression grew serious. "I suppose you are in a bit of a different situation from your friends. I hadn't thought about that."

It hadn't really hit Stephanie either until now. "Cassidy gets to ask Jace things as they come up. And Stacy has been learning tons from Del, especially as he's been teaching Colt about being a wolf after all those years of muddling through on his own."

"You can always ask me."

It wasn't the words, it was the way he said it. As if it wasn't only a casual, *Hey, got a question? Let me help you with that.* More intense.

More —

Stephanie twisted in her seat. She examined his face as that little bubble inside her bounced all the way down to the base of her stomach and started doing a rapid jig. She liked Blue.

She. *Liked*. Blue.

His gaze was still on the road as they wound their way up the mountainside. It wasn't the kind of casual driving where you could shoot the breeze and have your attention everywhere, but somehow even though his eyes were straight forward, Stephanie felt as if he were highly tuned to her. Maybe even aware of the bubbling sensation she wasn't sure how to deal with.

She turned to focus straight ahead as well. Because even coming to realize that maybe things had changed inside her, when it came to this man, nothing had really changed. He was—

He was a good man. There was no other way of saying it, and she knew that the semantics were wrong because he wasn't a man at all.

But still, he was always there for everyone. Rock solid and lighthearted and just honest and kind. And she wasn't about to try and get involved—whatever *that* ended up meaning—with somebody that good and solid and wonderful when she knew what she was.

Which was exactly the *opposite* of wonderful, no matter how much she hid under a bubbly façade. The stain on her hands was proof of her inner badness.

Blue pointed ahead of them. "Moving on from the teeth comment, that's our next turn. We will be taking a momentary pit stop at this point because whatever else wants to rattle loose, my bladder needs to be empty for however long the next portion of the journey continues."

He pulled off the side of the road, and they headed into the trees on either side of the truck. It was a good idea, Stephanie supposed.

Ten minutes later she was immensely grateful that he'd had the foresight to suggest the break. She clutched the *oh shit* handle above her head, braced one hand on the center console and, despite Blue inching his way forward on the road, she still felt as if she was being tossed in a rock tumbler. "This road makes no sense."

"When you consider your artist absolutely hates public interaction, this road makes a whole lot of sense," Blue assured her.

"How does he get supplies in? Does he run them in as a cat? I doubt he's hauling canvas and wood frames up this road on a regular basis," she complained.

Blue chuckled softly. "You are talking about François Andean. Chances are he gets things helicoptered in."

"Oh. True." She sighed heavily. "Too bad my budget doesn't run to helicoptering the paintings out."

"Too bad," Blue agreed. He eased the front wheels around another massive rock then shrugged. "It's been a while, but I seem to remember stretches of the road are better. As if he lets parts of it nearly wash away to discourage visitors. The other parts are only horrible instead of god-awful."

Stephanie was exhausted by the time they caught the first glimpse of the cabin ahead of them. Holding herself steady in the constantly shifting and shaking vehicle had involved every single muscle in her body. "*I'm* going to need a massage by the time we get down the hill."

"I can help with that," Blue said casually then lifted a finger and pointed. "Creek crossing, and then we'll be able to stand on solid ground."

He inched his way through the running water. Stephanie rolled down the window and stared in amazement as the running boards were covered briefly before the Jeep rose back to dry land.

Blue pulled to a stop outside the larger barn-shaped building. Stephanie eased open her door and crawled out, groaning as her feet hit the ground. "Is that an earthquake? Is the world shaking?"

Blue approached cautiously from around the Jeep, grinning as he took careful steps as well. "Trust me, my wolf is seriously pissed at me right now. He cannot understand why anyone would want to experience that drive when we could've just run."

Stephanie stood with one hand on the door as she waited for her legs to stabilize. "Ask your wolf how he planned to get a dozen paintings down the mountain. As bumpy as it was, thank goodness we have the Jeep."

They stood quietly for a moment. Stephanie stared admiringly at the mountain tops soaring around them. The barn and the cabin were built from log timbers, perfectly set into the ancient forest. The scent of fall surrounded them, and larch trees turning yellow were dotted here and there in the meadow. Mountain peaks to the left held back a thick row of lofty high clouds with darkness at their centers, but directly above her head, the sky was a mix of brilliant blue and puffy white. It was an amazing location, albeit extremely remote.

Heavenward, a bald eagle circled lazily, wings extended as it floated on the air currents. A lone sentinel surveying its wilderness kingdom.

She lowered her gaze to find Blue watching her. The bubble in her stomach reactivated, jigging up and down in the center of her chest. She might not know everything that was going on, and she might not be able to act on the strange, wonderful sensation growing inside, but this much she knew. This much she needed to share. "I'm glad you're the one who brought me here."

~

Soon. Soon. Soon. His wolf whispered the words with complete conviction.

Blue considered asking for more information, but more important was the moment in front of him. The delight in Stephanie's eyes as she met his gaze firmly.

"I'm glad I get to do these things with you," he shared back.

Stephanie flung her arms out to the sides and rotated in a circle, head tilted back toward the sky, and he watched, gaze drifting over her lush curves and happy features.

Okay, not getting to follow through on the mating connection sucked, but there was a kind of joy in knowing that someday—possibly soon—this amazing woman would be his to cherish and love.

For now, the best way to do that was to simply enjoy time with her. Blue stretched his arms to either side and copied her, moving slowly at first and then increasing speed until he was whirling like a dervish. His wolf, unable to remain silent, got into the act. A howl slid past his human throat that sounded weak to his wolf's ears, but whatever. He did it again with delight.

When his feet tangled together and he went down in a crashing heap, Stephanie laughed and rushed to his side, hand held out to help him up. "You don't have to go quite so fast next time."

Blue chuckled. "You assume there will be a next time."

"There's always a next time," Stephanie said seriously. Then she rubbed her hands together and tilted her head toward the house. "Shall we go see if my artiste is here?"

As it turned out, François had already abandoned the premises. He'd left a note pinned to the front door with a paring knife.

Stephanie. Sorry I'm not there to help you, but my cougar needed to run. I left the paintings on the dining room table, and the larger canvases are in the studio. Since I didn't know what vehicle you'd bring, I haven't packaged them, but what you need is available. Use all the packing tape and boxes you need.

There is food in the refrigerator. If I can be so bold as to ask you to take anything that would rot with you when you go, that will mean less of a mess when I finally return.

When I'm back, I'll come to the lodge to see where you have put my work for others to enjoy.

I did one additional painting as a present for you. That one is wrapped. Presents should always be wrapped, don't you think? Unwrapping is so much fun.

Blue tried the door of the cabin, and it opened easily. He took a deep breath, scenting the air, but caught nothing except the fading trace of a male cougar.

Blue stepped back to let Stephanie walk in ahead of him.

Like many mountain cabins, the interior held an interesting mix of darkness and light. The wood timbers had aged to a deep honey gold, and with limited windows in this first section of the cabin, the daylight barely snuck into the deep corners.

A neat row of hooks with a shoe rack underneath lay to the side of the door. To the left was a kitchen area with the sink in front of the small window, miles of countertop, and a large island. All of it neatly tucked into a fifteen-by-fifteen space.

"Not bad for a rustic cabin," Blue said.

Stephanie walked through the room and into the gap at the end of the kitchen then whistled softly. "Wow. Rustic cabin, my ass."

Blue stepped beside her, trying really hard to not think about said ass when it was right there, conveniently at hand grasping height. And then his gaze shot over the newly exposed room and his whistle joined hers. "Holy shit. This is spectacular."

As if the entrance way and kitchen had been a false front, playing up the good old rustic cabin theme, this room turned that on its head and spiraled all the way up past spectacular to awe-inspiring.

Part of that was the view. The far wall of the room, which lay a good twenty-five feet away from where they stood, was made up almost entirely of glass. Wooden beams reached from floor to ceiling as the support posts, but in between each of them were an assortment of glass panes. Different sizes, different shapes. A few were filled with stained glass mosaics. But the effect was stunning and light filled.

The light fell on a massive dining room table and a fireplace against the north wall made of huge river rocks. The mantle looked to be a half plank made from one of the forest giants. Two comfortable leather recliners sat on either side of a leather loveseat directly in front of the fireplace, and along the opposite wall were a series of bookcases and knickknack collections as well as some of the artist's work.

Stephanie walked forward as if in a daze, trailing her fingers over the furniture until she was pressed against the glass and staring down into the valley. "How is this even possible? I know we came up the mountain, and I saw another peak off to the left, but I didn't see this view from where we parked the Jeep."

"Location, location, location." Blue was equally astonished and impressed. "There's a forest of trees to the east of where we parked. Somehow that hid the ridge we're looking at now."

The house was perched in the very center of a narrow tableland, with the peak to the left and another in the distance to the right. Below them, swooping down before rising again, was a deep valley, tree-lined and beautiful. The faintest hint of sparkle at the base suggested a river ran through it.

Stephanie leaned against Blue's side, her head on his shoulder. "I'm very glad you made us get up early, because I have a feeling this view is going to distract me. I haven't even looked at the paintings François made for us."

Blue rested a hand lightly on her waist, holding her against him because it felt so right. "We have time," he assured her. "Also, I imagine François has no problems with you coming up for a visit a time or two. Not if he's making you presents."

He wasn't quite sure what to think of that part. A hit of jealousy was beat down immediately. Stephanie needed friends in her life, and that's what François was. A friend.

He *hoped* that was all the man was thinking of, or there would a very firm future meeting between Blue's wolf and François's cougar.

She stepped away, gaze still lingering out the window. "Okay. Let's look at what he's got here, then go to the studio and check the paintings there. I asked for three large and a half dozen small-to-medium works. You can help me decide how we should package them so they'll fit in the Jeep."

"Sounds like a plan."

They moved together to the dining room table. "François has only one chair at the table," Stephanie said, a hint of sadness in her voice. "I knew he was a loner, but that seems extreme."

"Cougar shifters tend to like their space," Blue pointed out. He stopped beside the table and glanced down. "Wow. Again, maybe he's some kind of magician as well as shifter. These are incredible."

Stephanie leaned over the table, lightly touching the frame of the painting in front of her. "He's used pinecone pieces to make the fur of the wolf three-dimensional in this one. And he somehow layered the paint of the mountain in the background, so it looks as if this is a photograph."

"Mixed media, and a lot of the media are natural objects. He really is a master-level artist." Blue scanned the rest of the table. "I think François really likes you. You asked for a half dozen paintings, and he's given you twice as many."

Stephanie counted as she recited. "Four landscapes, four wild animal scenes, and four rivers. They're beautiful." She flashed a grin at Blue and grabbed his hand. "Come on. I can't wait to see what he did with the big canvases."

He went with her to the door, bumping into her back when she stopped one step outside on the porch. Both of them looked up toward the western mountains where the clouds had been clinging to the very top as if held back by the cliffs.

They weren't held back anymore. The wind picked up and pushed the ominous black thunderheads toward their meadow at a speed appropriate to an apocalyptic movie.

"Uh-oh. That doesn't look good," Stephanie said as a ragged bolt of silvery-blue shot across the sky.

"Flash storm. We're about to get a whole lot of rain," Blue agreed.

He didn't need to add the part about the temperature dropping. The cool wind turned icy as it slapped their skin with a warning.

Blue knew these mountains. Knew what a sudden storm at this time of year could do. Their chances of getting down the mountain today just grew extremely unlikely.

5

The rumble of thunder shook the air over them, and Stephanie shivered.

Memories had flashed in along with the lightning. A stark white face with staring eyes. Crimson blood splashed everywhere—so, so much blood. Her palms itched, and she scrubbed her hands together as another ear-rattling noise broke from the sky.

She pushed away the nightmare and cursed softly. "If we leave now, we can make it down the hill in time?"

Blue didn't have to answer, the sky did it for him. Between one breath and the next, raindrops, huge and heavy, slammed into the deck at their feet like the slow pound of hammers.

He tugged her against him, back under the eaves. "We can't drive in this. Some sections of the road will turn slick with mud. But others are unstable enough they could simply slide away and take us with them."

Another flash of lightning lit up the sky, the roar on the air hitting an instant later. The porch shook under their feet, and the scent of ozone, sharp and terrible, filled her nostrils.

A strong hand on her arm guided her back into the cabin. Blue squeezed tight before letting go. "The storm is directly over us. Let's get somewhere safe. Also known as away from the windows and the fireplace."

"The fireplace?" She hurried after him as he led the way back into the massive living space. "Really?"

"If the place is well constructed, which it probably is, we don't need to worry." He pointed to the side wall and a door she hadn't even noticed on their first trip. A staircase led into darkness. Blue flipped a switch to find them light then led her downward, continuing his story. "An old cabin I stayed in once went up in flames after a lightning strike. The miner who built it had repurposed junk he gathered from the river. Including a lovely bit of metal he used as a cornerstone. Ran all the way from the top of the chimney to the cabin floor, and when it got hit, *poof*."

"Shish-kabob wolves?"

"No casualties, but singed fur is not a pleasant aroma, that I can tell you." Blue stopped at the bottom landing and took a deep breath. "Just as I thought. Living quarters are tucked down here."

"It's quiet," Stephanie pointed out. "Did the storm pass that quickly?"

"Your friend built into the hillside. We're currently underground, mostly. Trust me, it's still dumping buckets out there." Blue flipped another set of switches then whistled.

An extremely long hallway sat to their left. Stephanie counted four doors, all widely spaced apart. "That's a lot of bedrooms for a loner."

Blue swung open the closest door but refrained from

stepping into the room. "This one is François' bedroom. Sweet view—the same as from the living room, but lower—and there's a bathroom to the side."

"Let's not go in," Stephanie offered quickly. "No need, and he probably wouldn't like our scent in there."

She marched to the next door and peeked in. "Laundry. Nothing over the top but very efficient. Front load wash and dry, room to hang to dry. Massive sink."

"Our boy likes his creature comforts." Blue was at the next door, and this time amusement rose. "Oh, he likes his creature comforts very much."

She peered over Blue's shoulder. "Wine cellar. Isn't that supposed to be somewhere in the bowels of the castle?"

"No windows, temperature controlled..." Blue slipped in and peered at one of the dusty shelves with bottles stored on their sides. "This is as castle-like as you can get. I really need to meet this man. I think we're going to be besties. He's an artistic genius, and his taste in liquor is amazing."

Stephanie slapped Blue's finger's lightly as he reached for a bottle. "No touching. No scent, remember?"

Blue made a face. "No scent in *his* room, I agree with. But we're stuck for at least twenty-four hours. I am certainly touching a bottle of wine. Something to go with the meal we'll make from his leftovers."

"Let's hope there's more than pickles in the fridge." Stephanie eyed the wall. That made sense. "Okay, but I'm buying another of whatever you grab and replacing it, so don't go too fancy."

"My treat." Blue flashed her a smile that made the butterflies all quiver for a reason other than the storm. "Last door."

No reason it had to be a bedroom. Loner cougar? "I bet it's a gym," Stephanie guessed as they approached the door.

A snort escaped Blue. "What are the stakes of this bet? Because it's absolutely not a gym. The guy has the entire mountain outside his door, and he's a cougar. It's a bedroom."

"Loser has to give the winner a foot massage," Stephanie proposed, thrusting her hand at Blue.

He took it instantly. "Deal. My feet could use some TLC."

They shook, then she pushed the door open.

Floor to ceiling windows once again showcased the view, and Stephanie got caught up by the distraction. "Look at that," she said in a worshipful whisper, stepping forward as if pulled by a magnet.

The storm raged, raindrops slamming into the window. The sky roiled with black and grey, and it was awe-inspiring and amazing and...

A tortured laugh, semi-snort, nearly giggle rose behind her. She twisted on the spot to find Blue staring intently at the ceiling, his shoulders shaking, tears pouring down his cheeks.

"Are you okay?" she demanded, abandoning the view and rushing to his side.

He couldn't talk and didn't seem to be breathing much except for a few wheezing gasps. He lifted a hand and pointed away from the window that had caught her attention to the center of the room.

A bed took up fifty percent of the center of the space. Crimson red sheets with pure white linens and pillows piled high. Very opulent, very round.

Blue adjusted his quivering pointer finger toward the ceiling to make sure she didn't miss the mirrors.

Drat. There went her bet.

"Okay, so it's a bedroom." Steph's gaze kept roving,

but she patted Blue lightly on the back because he still wasn't breathing properly. "I don't know why you're carrying on like this. I'm sure there's a rule that *every* mountain cabin must have a massive round bed with mirrors over it. And..." she stalled out. "Why is there a giant wooden frame in the shape of an X over there? And is that a..."

Blue collapsed to the ground, clutching his stomach as laughter spilled freely. "A spanking bench? I think so. And I think that's the hook up for a swing—a nudge-nudge, wink-wink type of swing."

It wasn't possible. Her online friend had never hinted at anything out of the ordinary. "He's got a sex dungeon in his cabin."

At her feet, Blue rolled to his side and pulled up to a seated position. His grin remained huge. "He's got a sex dungeon."

She looked around with curiosity. "I've never been to a place like this—never had the urge. Still, this means I win."

Blue shuffled to his feet. "What? It's more a bedroom than a gym."

"You said it's a dungeon. Dungeon, gym, same thing in my book," Stephanie said primly.

He considered, then nodded, amusement on his face. "You've got a point."

∼

BLUE HELD onto the sensation of laughter as hard as he could because it was far safer than giving his imagination free rein.

After three months of waiting, he had a very good imagination. A perfect image flashed to mind of that decadent, sensual bed with Stephanie stretched out, hair draped over her shoulder and nothing else covering her.

Or leaning on the St. Andrew's cross. He wasn't into hardcore dominance games, but damn, she'd look great spread eagle, heat in her eyes as she waited for him to tease her to ecstasy.

He clapped his hands together to stop from reaching for her. "I'm starving."

Truth, only it wasn't food he craved.

"Do you think it's safe to go upstairs?" Steph asked, following him from the room, close enough that her heat washed over him.

Safer than staying within sight of that bed. "We'll be careful. We really do need to check the supply situation, aka the fridge leftovers and pantry shelves. We could be stuck for a while."

"I'm glad we're together. Stace and Cassidy won't worry because they know you'll take care of me."

His wolf preened at the compliment. "Good. And I will. Take care of you," he promised.

Behave, behave, behave, he recited to himself as they returned to the kitchen.

Outside, the storm boomed away happily. Lightning flashed over and over, rattling sounds shaking the walls.

Steph folded her arms over her chest and made a face. "I used to like storms."

"It'll be okay." he promised again. Time for a distraction for them both. He gestured to the fridge. "Let's see what kind of pickle tray we're having with our wine tonight."

"Fine, lazybones. Not as if you couldn't reach out the extra two feet and open it yourself." But she took the hint and hauled open the fridge door then jerked to a stop. "Oh. My."

"What?" Blue leaned over her shoulder, pressing to her back, bodies in light contact. Yes. He had to be this close to see what was going on.

Liar.

She pulled a tray off the top shelf. It was wrapped up with that crinkly decorative cellophane stuff that people used on gift baskets. "This isn't leftovers. This has my name on it."

An uneasy sensation hit, and the hairs on the back of Blue's neck stood up. "How did you say you met this guy again?"

"François? I saw his art online and we started corresponding. We've never met in person." She lowered the tray to the side counter and pulled the ribbon loose.

Chocolate-covered strawberries. Expensive cheese and sausage. A tin of some kind of fish. Teeny little pickles and pearly white onions.

Steph pointed at the tray. "You were right. Pickles."

She twisted toward him with delight in her eyes, and Blue forced a smile. "I'm surprised they're not chocolate covered, too. What a missed opportunity."

"Ugh. There's a taste sensation I'm not up for trying." Stephanie left the tray there and returned to the fridge. "It's nice that he wanted to leave me something for the bother of coming up here to grab the paintings. I hope there's some real food, though."

Poking through the freezer, they found enough meat and veggies that Blue was no longer worried about starving. Just very, very uneasy about the *gift for Stephanie* situation. Not knowing what was going on made him twitchy.

Steph wandered away from him farther along the inner wall, pulling cupboards open. "I'll make sandwiches if we can find some peanut butter."

Blue pulled out the frozen loaf of bread they'd found. "That's a solid plan. I spotted a deck of cards. We can play for who does dishes."

She snorted. "So many dishes, after making sandwiches."

"Knives, spoons, plates, frying pans." She gave him a look and he winked. "Kidding. We don't need the spoons."

Blue had nearly regained his equilibrium when the strong scent of cat drifted through his system. He whirled, expecting to find François staring them down.

Instead, he discovered a wrapped painting about two feet by four feet propped against the far side of the island. Hidden in plain sight, as it were.

Stephanie's name was on the label, and another rush of uncertainty struck.

Before Blue could do anything with his gut feeling of impending doom, she was beside him. "Oh. That's the present François said he left. He didn't need to do that."

She slid it onto the island and tugged at the twine binding it together.

The string loosened instantly, uncurling from the package as if magic were involved. The front paper fluttered away, and suddenly a multi-layered image appeared.

A single glance was enough to make Blue see red.

The outside edges showed deep forest with many types of trees and lush green underbrush. Off-center, a small clearing cut through the wilderness, the sun shining in like a spotlight to highlight the main feature.

A cougar lay in the beam of sunshine, musculature frame accented by the shadows formed on his body. An extraordinary creature, the big cat's head rested in the lap of a human.

His human. *Blue's—*

Because it was most definitely meant to be Stephanie on the canvas. The woman's colouring was the same, her hair arranged the way Steph liked to drape her hair over her right shoulder. The familiar position of the relaxed feminine body—legs crossed at the ankle, leaning back on her arms, face lifted to the sky.

Maybe he was jumping to conclusions. A million people liked that position, but this was Stephanie to the core.

Why is our mate in this picture? his wolf asked, clearly perplexed. *Why is she with another shifter?*

It was one of the most uncomfortable dual-personality moments Blue had ever experienced. He always knew what his other half was thinking, but he was only one being—the wolf a part of him, not a separate individual. But right now, he truly felt as if his wolf was separate from him and asking him the question.

No, *demanding.*

That's our *mate. He is trying to woo* our *mate.* A feral growl ripped from Blue's lips, and Stephanie eyed him with concern.

As she should. His wolf was a second away from taking control and turning them furry.

Blue opened and closed his hands a few times, fighting for control.

"Blue?" Steph leaned closer, even as she shuffled a half-step back. Some part of her subconscious registering that the wild animal beside her was dangerous. "Are you okay?"

He stared at the picture as his claws extended through his fingertips. Patience. Waiting. All the things that he'd been doing for months fell away in a blaze of inner fury.

One hand flew forward. He wasn't in charge of the motion. He'd kept from shifting, but the wolf was not fucking around. Claws at full extension, Blue made a swipe at the canvas as he turned to fully face Steph.

It's time. Now. Now, now, now his wolf demanded.

She met his gaze straight on. Thank God he didn't see fear in her eyes, but there was confusion. "I take it you don't like the gift François gave me."

"He's trying to woo you. But he can't." A growl full of frustration and fury.

"I didn't ask him to," she offered peacefully. "I don't want him to."

"That's good. But he's still trying, and it's not happening." Blue's voice crackled between human and howl. "Because you're *my* mate."

6

____

 *ou're my mate.*

 Blood rushed from her head to her toes. *"What?"*

Blue pressed his palms to the sides of her shoulders, bracing her because she'd swayed. "Shit. Didn't mean to say that out loud."

"But you said it because you think it's true." She didn't make it a question because it was clear that was not the kind of statement any wolf would joke about. That much she'd picked up on her own while everybody else was getting lessons in wolfdom.

He dipped his chin in agreement.

An icy chill ran up her spine just as she became aware of the claw tips pressing into the backs of her arms. "Blue, did you know your claws are out?"

"Sorry. I'm working on it."

"Work faster," she said softly. Then, because he really was a good friend and even during this chaos, she didn't want him to worry, she added, "I'm not really scared by the claws, but I know it's the kind of thing that would bother you."

He bobbed his head a few times as he made a shitty attempt at a smile. He rubbed the palms of his hands gently up and down her arms, claws well away from her skin. "Not the time and place I planned to make that announcement."

Her mind had been whirling through everything she knew about wolves. "This isn't a recent development for you, is it?"

The direction of his head motion flipped from up and down then side to side. Still more aggressive than it needed to be. "Nope."

Shit, shit, shit. Stephanie pressed her hands to his chest, partly to have another point of stability and partly so she could pet him gently. "Okay. I think we need to have a sit-down talk, but do you need to run off some energy first? Need me to make those sandwiches? How do we make this better for you?"

He swallowed hard. "You saying *yippee!* and declaring your eternal love is probably out of the question, yes?"

A hard thump smacked inside her chest. "Definitely a little too optimistic for the moment. But sandwiches I can do, and then we can sit over there and talk."

Blue stepped away from her, hands falling to his sides, claws retracting the slightest bit. "I'll let you put the peanut butter on the bread." He held a hand up and stared at his fingertips sheepishly. "I have used utensils like this, but it's not pretty."

Stephanie retreated to the counter where the jar of peanut butter and loaf of bread waited. Behind her, Blue was rummaging through cupboards, so she ignored him as best she could and focused instead on smoothing the exact amount of peanut butter on every single piece of bread. Sliding to the corners, neat and precise. Calm. Cool.

The exact opposite of what was going on inside of her. She was his mate? What the heck was she supposed to do with that?

Part of his confession made her want to dance and sing. She liked him. She *really* liked him, even after three months. Maybe because for those three months it had been the two of them working together, playing together, being together. Which was exactly what Stephanie needed when it came to forming connections. It was the other parts that worried her.

Mates had no secrets.

Another dab of peanut butter on the bread. Intense focus on the task at hand as a jumble of images from the past poured through her, bloody and harsh. Having a good friend in her life. Having a mate who, according to all the wolf rules, would be there for her forever.

That part didn't sound bad. The part that made her spine stiffen was that he would then know what she'd done.

And that could not happen.

Stephanie cut all the sandwiches carefully then loaded them onto a plate. She turned to discover Blue already seated at the small rustic table in the corner of the room. He'd put two glasses on the surface and was pouring golden liquid into them.

She dropped the plate of food between them. "Day drinking, are we?"

Blue lifted his tumbler in a salute to her. "It seemed appropriate."

She raised her glass, and they clinked them together. Stephanie took a sip, and the whiskey burned a path down her throat, smooth but sharp.

Across from her, Blue tipped back the glass and swallowed it in one gulp.

She raised a brow. "Good thing for wolf metabolism."

"Very good thing." Blue put his glass down and pressed his palms to the table. Fully human hands again, she noted with approval. "It's not as if I can take it back, and it's not as if I want to. But it changes nothing."

She laughed. When he met her gaze, confusion in his eyes, she matched his position. Leaning forward, palms pressed the table surface. "I call bullshit, Blue. You can't just up and tell me that we're mates and then say oh, but it changes nothing. You don't want us to continue the way we were."

"No," he agreed grudgingly.

Tough move, what to say next. "This is like you always agreeing to everything that I say. I need you to tell me what you actually want."

"I kinda did," Blue pointed out. "The whole *pledging your eternal love* comment was not a joke."

"But you're smart enough to know that's not going to happen. Not this instant. So what does this all mean?" Stephanie picked up a sandwich for something to do with her hands. "Remember, I haven't been getting the wolf lessons. From what I've seen from my friends, their matings went differently. Cassidy has this whole wolf guru, mystical-mental stuff that connects her with Jace. My sister and Delaney were dream walking together. We don't have any of that stuff."

Blue lifted his shoulders and grabbed a sandwich himself. "I don't have the answers to this one. I've never had a mate before. I wanted one—I want *you*. I don't know what mating is going to look like for us."

"You guys really need to work on the *Everything You*

Need to Know About Werewolves encyclopedia. It would come in handy."

"It would be really dangerous," Blue pointed out. "It would probably also not be very helpful, because as far as I can tell, every mated couple seems to have their own gig. And I don't know any other Omegas. Wait, that's bullshit. I do know other Omegas, but not close enough to be friends who share details of their relationship stuff."

Stephanie nodded and silently ate her sandwich. Thinking hard.

She *liked* Blue, which was a very important component for her. More important for her than for many other people. And while the whole idea of being intimately mind-connected and mated was still hugely in the *no* category, maybe there would be a workaround.

Like being super-besties. Almost, but not quite mates.

While she'd been silent, Blue slowly worked on the pile of sandwiches. He held his body upright in a ready-for-action position, his rainbow-coloured shirt covering broad shoulders and a muscular torso.

She let her gaze drift over him and really thought hard about what it would mean to be with a man like him. Was she interested?

The fact the answer was *yes* sent both relief and a hint of panic through her. It removed one reason to simply turn him down. But it also gave her a place to start the next stage of the conversation.

She waited until he'd finished swallowing. She took another sip of her own whiskey for courage and then cleared her throat. "You need to know something about me."

His attention snapped back on her. The way that it always had been, she realized now. Focused, intent. Caring, as if what she was about to say was of vital importance to him. "Yes?"

"I'm demisexual."

~

HE'D HEARD the word before, but he wasn't sure what it meant in this context. He wasn't up on all the bits and pieces of sexual identity discussed in the media, mostly because it really didn't matter to him. Between consenting adults, fun was fun.

But this was obviously uber-important to her, which meant he needed to know more. From the crease between her brows, it meant something to the situation between them. Which, thankfully, didn't seem to be coming out as a straight up *absolutely no* on her part. "What does demisexual mean?"

She sighed. "It means when people joke about sex, or they're talking about *whooo, look at that hot guy on the street*, it goes over my head. Sex talk doesn't interest me. Like, watching porn is totally boring because there's no plot, and I have no emotional attachment to anybody on the screen, so it's like some weird nature show with the sexual habits of humans."

Blue sat back in his chair. "No sex. You don't...like sex."

Her firm gaze faltered, and to his surprise a rosy flush covered her cheeks. "That's not what it means. I do like sex. As it turns out, I like it quite a bit, but only with people I really trust and know well as a friend. Otherwise I don't feel attracted to them, no matter how good-looking or sexy they are."

His mind rushed through the details of what she had

said earlier. "Only with people you have an emotional attachment to."

"Yes." She continued to avoid his gaze, now picking at the crust of a sandwich she obviously did not plan on eating.

Okay, it was a bit self-serving to be hugely relieved that he wasn't about to live an entirely platonic lifestyle with his mate. Or at least he hoped that was where this conversation was leading. "And are you anywhere near to having an emotional attachment to me?"

Her gaze snapped up, and she offered him a dirty look. "Please."

Blue held his hands in the air. "Just wanted to clarify. Pretty important detail in a long-term relationship. Although it's only a part of the whole package."

A snort escaped her. "I get it."

Blue pushed aside the plate of sandwiches and caught Stephanie's hands. Her fingers were warm, and she instantly tangled them together with his. Here was something he could give her. A truth that might make a difference in the next thing that happened between them. "The first minute I met you, my wolf said you would be my mate"—worry drifted into her gaze—"but not yet."

Her head tilted to the side, her hair sliding over her shoulder. "Smart wolf. Because I didn't like you."

"Oh, you liked me. You know you did. Everybody likes me," Blue teased to lighten the situation.

Stephanie's smile warmed. "You're a very likable guy. This is true."

It all made so much more sense now. "You didn't *like* me in the right way. But now you do."

She glanced at the picture that he'd clawed where it leaned against the side wall. He'd made a very precise slash against the canvas, leaving the image of Stephanie untouched and the cougar in ribbons.

She motioned with her chin because he refused to let her fingers free. "I'm a little perturbed by that."

"Not one of my finer moments," Blue agreed. "Can I blame it on my wolf? He really doesn't like your François right now."

Stephanie refocused on him. Heat sparked from her eyes in warning. "He's not *my* François. Plus, I didn't do anything to encourage him, and I never gave him a picture of me to put into that painting. Because I'm not dumb, and I do see what he's done there."

"So, logical conclusion, you also see what he must have been up to?"

She sighed heavily. "Stalking me?"

Another uncomfortable feeling shot through Blue as his wolf's hackles rose at the thought of somebody hanging around Timberwolf Lodge spying on her. "I'm upping security at the lodge. And someone needs to have a firm talk with François."

Stephanie slipped her hands from his so she could shake a finger in his face. "That will be me. But you can be there," she added instantly, ruining all his protests.

That was only the first part of this conversation. They were nowhere near a final understanding on the most important matter of his entire life.

He leaned back in his chair, giving her some space. "Stephanie."

"Blue." She copied his position, mirroring him back. She even crossed her arms over her chest, although on her it just framed that perfect pair of breasts which caused interesting reactions in his body.

"You are very important to me," Blue shared. "Yes,

because my wolf says we are potentially each other's forever. But also because over the past few months I have gotten to like you as well."

Her smile softened. "Awww. That's sweet."

"What would make moving toward being mates work for you?"

Look at him being all polite and restrained. Especially when he knew his own agenda was something primitive along the lines of strip her down, fuck her brains out, and bite her.

She hesitated. "It's not that you aren't a good guy. And I'll be blunt and say the idea of fooling around with you is attractive. But I'm not very keen on the whole mating thing. It's just not for me."

"I'm not asking for it today," Blue said with infinite patience, suddenly sure that this was exactly what needed to happen. "But I hope that you will stay open to the idea. And maybe at some point we'll find our own mystical, woo-woo magic. Who knows what will develop between the two of us? That's what I hope you'll give a chance. That you'll give *us* a chance to become whatever we're supposed to be."

The reluctance in her eyes turned hopeful. "I like you, Blue. I like being with you because you're funny, and you're smart, and you make me laugh. So do I want to keep spending time with you? Absolutely."

"But more than time together like we have been, yes? We can take this to the next stage?" Blue couldn't help it; a snort of laughter escaped. "I have never felt more human than in this moment. God, wolves don't date their mates."

Her smile was back. The real one that went all the way through her. "Go on. Do the whole human experience. It's good for you to understand how the other half works."

Blue stood then held a hand to her as she rose to her feet as well. "Stephanie Nix, would you go steady with me?"

Her lips twitched. "God, for a second there I thought you were going to ask me to shack up with you."

He put on a horrified expression. "I might be easy, but I am not that kind of wolf."

Laughter bubbled up, and then Stephanie closed the gap between them. She rested her hands on his shoulders, shining eyes staring intently into his. She considered, pondered.

He could have stood there all day because she was pressed up against him, and holy hell, it felt good.

But then the best possible thing happened. She said yes.

"We can date. And we'll get to know each other better. And we'll see what happens with this magical, woo-woo, mystical, rah-rah, Omega wolfieness. But mostly, we'll be friends."

He rested his hands on her hips, preparing to pull her in for a hug. "That sounds great."

She slid her hands from his shoulders and locked them behind his neck as she went up on her toes. "Friends who now kiss."

7

———

She was flying entirely on gut instinct at that point. But as she leaned into Blue and pressed their lips together, she was pretty damn sure her instincts were correct.

A soft caress, her lips over his. The taste of the air he breathed, wilderness and mountains in the flavour, sliding over her cheek. She teased her tongue into his mouth, flicking briefly against his.

A low groan rumbled up from deep in his chest, and his hands tightened on her hips.

The front of their bodies connected—her breasts against the broad muscles of that admittedly impressive chest. The hardening length of his cock to her belly. And Stephanie angled her head to the side to try and connect a little more.

His grip tightened, and her feet left the floor. Instinctively, she wrapped her legs around him, and a moment later she was pressed against the nearest wall with Blue totally in charge of the kiss.

In charge of holding her levitated in midair, pinned in place by a slab of muscular male dressed in a kaleidoscope of colours. And what was her brain doing thinking about what the man chose to wear when his tongue and teeth were doing wicked things to her mouth?

He nipped her lower lip, and Stephanie gasped. It hadn't hurt so much as sent a lightning bolt from her mouth directly to her core. It was as if the storm that continued to rage outside had shot a small version of itself into the room. A crackle of pleasure rolled over her skin. The breaking sound of his groan as his lips moved from her mouth across her jaw and into the dip where her neck met her shoulder.

A flash of light hit behind her eyes as he sucked, and every inch of her lit up with pleasure. "Blue," she moaned.

"I don't want to stop," he confessed between kisses, still attacking her neck with unrelenting ecstasy. "Touching you. Tasting you—it's like nothing I've ever experienced before."

Stephanie tightened her legs, and the ridge of her jeans ground against his hard-on. They both moaned, and again when Blue lifted and lowered her slightly, intensifying the sensation.

She let go of the death grip she'd had on his shoulders, cupped his face, and brought their mouths back together because she hadn't had enough of this. Tasting him. Touching him.

Blue stepped away from the wall, their mouths still connected as he walked blindly back to the table. The next thing she knew he was seated in a sturdy kitchen chair with her draped over him, legs on either side of his trim hips.

It made it easier to keep kissing. She slipped her hands down his chest, opening buttons and pushing the fabric aside so she could connect her palms to the bare skin she discovered. She scratched lightly, and Blue moaned. The heat of him was scalding and addictive, and Stephanie found herself panting for air when he separated their lips.

She could only imagine what they looked like at that moment. His hair stuck up in every direction as if they'd been tussling in bed for hours. One shoulder of his shirt hung off, the front of the material gaping open and a line of four red marks from her fingernails were clearly visible across his chest.

Whoops. Maybe she hadn't scratched as lightly as she'd thought.

Her hair hung in her eyes, her T-shirt untucked and scrunched up on one side where his hand still rested against her bare waist.

They grinned at each other. Blue swept a finger up and down against her skin, but he didn't make a move to go back to kissing or try to do anything more, and it was...

Right.

"I liked that," Stephanie admitted.

"I am so glad to hear you say that." If anything, his smile got bigger. "Okay if I plan to do a lot of that in the coming days?"

She nodded. "I know it might not seem like it considering I just about jumped your bones, but it's probably good if we mostly go slow."

"Time to get to know each other in a brand-new way. I get it."

Somehow she needed to navigate between the two things. The sense of absolute rightness of being with him and the total fear of discovery.

Giving a mental shrug, she decided that was a problem for down the road. After all, his wolf had said that they would be mates eventually. There was a long time between now and then.

In the meantime, she would find a way not to ruin this good, sweet man with the stains of her past.

Blue pushed her hair behind her ear. "Changing the subject. The storm is still pretty big, so we won't get out to the studio. Let's look at the pictures and start doing some packaging."

"We have to take that picture with us, you realize." She pointed to the one that he'd somehow managed to, without even looking at the actual canvas, slice and dice François away from her.

"I would apologize for ruining your gift, but I'd be absolutely lying." Blue glanced at the image and snarled. Then he cleared his throat and looked almost embarrassed. "My wolf is really pissed about that picture."

"So it appears." She'd seen his wolf many times, but this whole idea of being mates changed things up again. "Before we start packing, I have a favour to ask."

"I would say *anything*, but I have been taught a lesson by someone far smarter than me. Stephanie, what do you want help with?"

His answer was so perfect she tapped him on the nose. "I want to talk to your wolf."

He blinked. "Really?"

"Of course, really. I've seen your wolf a lot of times." She narrowed her gaze. "Why? Do you not think it's a good idea?"

Blue looked almost sheepish for a moment. "Just a heads up. He's acting weird. Like far more independent and not me, but he'd never do anything to hurt you." That last part he said with absolute conviction.

Stephanie uncurled herself from where she sat in his lap, standing beside him and offering her hand. "Well, then, maybe he just needs a chance to talk to me himself."

Blue shrugged the rest of the way out of his shirt, undid his zipper, and stripped away his pants and boxers in one move. He stood there and damn near preened under her gaze.

Good. Heavens. The man was ripped. Broad through the chest and shoulders with a narrow waist and hips. Muscles flexed along the sides of his torso and ran down to his groin area where she was most definitely not staring at his erection.

Nope. Not staring at all.

Although it did take every bit of strength in her to continue the admiration journey down his thighs and over the flexed calf muscles that she'd like to put her teeth to and nip.

"I'm really liking this *friends with* situation we've decided to move into." Blue's deep raspy tones slid over her skin, velvet smooth.

She couldn't tear her gaze off his human body. "You'd better shift."

"Steph." He spoke softly, and she glanced up to meet his gaze. "We're going to be good together, you and me. I promise."

Before she could respond, he was once again performing magic. Transforming somehow from flesh and bone into fur and teeth.

BLUE DIDN'T REMEMBER a time when he couldn't reach the other part of himself. He didn't have any experience with what it was like to be fully human, so trying to compare the usual sensation and relationship between him and his wolf and what he felt right now was difficult.

When he'd been young, like most of the kids in the pack, he flipped between animal and human without thinking when he was in a safe situation. At home or around his pack mates, he'd played, learned, and gotten into all sorts of mischief.

He had always been in charge. And by that he meant him, the human, the thinking side that was a little more aware of protocols.

That was not what he had at the moment. No sir. The closest thing he could liken it to was being a passenger in a vehicle. And not him in the back seat behind Jace or his buddies. This was more as if someone unknown was driving and Blue sat in the farthest back seat of a fifteen passenger van. Or maybe shoved in the trunk of a car.

His wolf had control of *everything*.

It had to have something to do with him and Stephanie being mates, although neither Jace nor Del had mentioned any such weirdness with their partners. Then again, neither of them were Omegas.

Still, there wasn't much he could do about it except watch and learn. And thankfully, he knew his wolf side adored Stephanie, possibly even more than he did.

Which is why when she went to her knees in front of him and opened her arms, Blue didn't worry one bit. His wolf nudged up against her, brushing his chin over her shoulder and winding around her. Coating her in his scent, thank you very much.

"You're very soft," Stephanie said, fingers drifting through his fur.

He batted her with his nose before crouching slightly to show off his muscles. Behind her, one of the strands of canvas he'd created with his claws fluttered, and he snorted. The damn cougar only dreamed he had that much muscle on him. Wouldn't take long to have the bastard on the ground and Blue's teeth around his throat.

Stephanie laughed softly. "Oh, excuse me. When I said soft, I meant your fur. You're very strong."

From his back seat position, Blue really wished he could roll his eyes. His wolf though, ate up her complement like candy, curling up in front of her and pressing his shoulders back against her fingers for a good scratching. Which Stephanie obligingly provided.

"So you're the one who told the big guy that we'll be mates at some point." Stephanie curled a hand around his muzzle and twisted until she could look him in the eye. "I'm pretty sure you heard that we've agreed to date. Which means you need to be patient because things work differently for humans than they do for wolves. Got it?"

Normally this would be a very odd conversation, all things considered. Since Blue was the wolf, and the wolf was Blue. But it seemed she might be smarter than he was because his wolf sniffed Stephanie hard then lay down and rolled belly up.

"Big old softy."

Softy indeed. The belly scritches were very welcome to both Blue and his wolf.

For a few minutes they stayed like that. Blue hanging out and enjoying the cuddle time with his future mate. It *was* going to happen.

But finally, Stephanie adjusted position, rising to her feet. "You need to shift back," she informed him. "The storm isn't going anywhere, so we probably need to play some cards or something to pass the time. We also need to wrap up packages. I think I saw the supplies stashed along the hall. I'll grab us glasses of water and meet you there."

Blue, who was his wolf, but also not his wolf, sat quietly on the floor. His tail wagged madly as he watched her move through the kitchen, humming happily. Bouncing back from the shock of what he'd thrown at her like a pro.

It probably helped that she had spent the last three months in full-on wolf pack territory. Plus all those years of being auntie to a packless wolf child.

She stepped out of the room, and Blue gathered himself to change back to human.

Normally, it happened without effort. Just the thought —*time to shift* — and he would become his other self.

Only now, his wolf hesitated. Kept control.

Not too worried, yet, Blue watched from his back seat position, waiting to see what his animal side was up to. Horror rose when he realized that in the past couple of seconds his wolf had moved him across the room and now stood beside the painting that leaned against the wall. A second later, he lifted his leg and marked his territory all over the canvas.

Only then did his wolf march contentedly over to the pile of human clothing and give up the reins.

Blue shifted back to human, cursing under his breath as he scrambled into his clothing before looking for cleaning supplies.

8

____

It seemed to take Blue a long time to rejoin her, but Stephanie didn't mind. She'd lost all control back there and still had to figure out whether that was a good thing or a bad thing.

It most definitely was a thing. She had a *mate*.

Damn it, she wasn't supposed to have done that, but now it seemed beyond cruel to call them off. And she couldn't lie and say that she didn't *want* to be in a relationship with Blue, because that was absolutely untrue. It was all the other complicated stuff that she wasn't certain about.

Still, first things first. They were stuck on the mountain, ergo, she couldn't chat with her sis or Cassidy to brainstorm solutions to her dilemma. She had tried her phone, but there was absolutely no reception as suspected.

So it was time for an involuntary holiday. A bit of relaxing, a bit of packaging up the paintings and hoping that Blue didn't destroy any of the other ones.

Although, she wasn't really worried about that. It was

very clear that François had gone beyond the boundaries of propriety only with the painting she was in.

She gathered the packing supplies that were tucked to the side of the table and was figuring out the best way to wrap canvases when Blue finally rejoined her. "I've been thinking about these paintings and whether it will be creepy to have them up in the lodge, but I've decided that they are just fine," she announced.

Blue smelled like dish soap and sanitizer. A waft of the cleaning supplies drifted off him as he stood next to her and obediently reached out a hand to hold the twine in place on the first picture she was wrapping. "Is there some sort of tangled mental escapade you had to go through to come up with this answer?"

"Definitely." Stephanie turned to face him, leaning her hip against the table. "François obviously came down to the lodge at some point to find out what I look like. And that gift picture was absolutely pushing it too far. So it will not be going up anywhere at the lodge."

"Damn fucking right it won't," Blue muttered in a villainous tone before speaking up a lot more perkily. Totally fake. "Gee, shucks, that's too bad."

She snickered. "But he is a good artist, and all these paintings are exactly what we need for the lodge. And since there was no breaking of boundaries involved with them, I'm fine having these pictures up, especially after you and I together have a mature, adult, and rational discussion with François to tell him..." She paused.

Blue raised a brow.

Oh dear. This was diving in the deep end from the ten meter board. "Once we tell him that we're mates," she finished.

The faintest bit of tension eased out of him as she said the words. "I like that plan."

"We're still just practice mates," she reminded him.

His lips twitched, and he reached for the glass of water that she'd left for him on the table, lifting it toward his lips. He paused and then offered dryly, "*That's* what we're going to call it?"

"I don't think my sister would approve of us announcing to the kids that we're fuck buddies."

Blue choked on his water, backing up and barely keeping from tossing the glass all over the paintings on the table. She clicked her tongue and grabbed his hand to steady him. "Sorry. That was a little crude."

His grin blossomed. "You can call us anything you want as long as it's going to be true."

The hope and happiness in his eyes made her feel guilty. Part of it was accurate—she was interested in continuing to develop their physical relationship. It was the *more than* physical part she was worried about.

They worked on wrapping the rest of the paintings without any further distraction. Blue made general comments about the artistic ability François displayed, and he nodded happily as he pointed at one of the images. "That is exactly what that valley looks like. And it's not a place a lot of tourists get to. If I didn't want to tie François's tail in a knot, I think we would be friends."

"You've obviously got the same taste in women," she pointed out before *tsking* at him in annoyance. "Stop growling. I was joking."

"I know. It's not me." Blue raised his hands to the sides in an innocent gesture. "My wolf is super out of sorts still, and he's overreacting to everything. I'm sorry about that, but there's not much I can do."

"Maybe this is a good time for a wolf lesson." She creased the corners on the butcher paper and tucked in the sides on picture number ten. "When you turn into a wolf, are you still inside? Or are you more Blue wolf, while I'm talking to Blue human now."

He wrinkled his nose for a minute. "Normally your question wouldn't even make sense. We're shifters. One person, just with a human form and an animal one. Some things my human side does better, like holding forks and higher mathematics." He winked.

"I thought you said you sucked at math," she demanded

"It's been a very long time since I was in school," he offered. "I can do math, but I choose to leave it to those people who enjoy it far more. I'm kind and giving like that."

"That's the human side. I'd assume your wolf can do things better like sniff, and track, and hide out."

"He's not only animal instincts. I mean, *I'm* not only all animal when I'm an animal," Blue protested. "I still reason and think." He made another face. "For example, my wolf side instantly knows in a room who relates to who. Like family, or friendships. It's a little bit of a pack knowledge that's helpful to have."

"You said normally my question wouldn't make sense. Why does it make sense now?"

Blue stuck a couple extra pieces of tape on the package then placed it against the wall with the rest of them that were finished. Then he turned and gave her his full attention. "I don't know if it's right now because we're sort of mates—"

"Buddy mates," she offered.

His concern slipped into a grin. "Cute one. Okay, I don't know if it's because of that or because I'm an Omega and there's a bunch of woo-woo rules that encompass the things that I normally do, but my wolf is acting a lot different than I would normally encourage."

She tried reading between the lines. "That doesn't sound good. If you want to do something, and he wants to do something else, who wins?"

Again with the innocent *I don't know* shrug. "I'm making this up as I go along," he admitted. Then he stepped forward and tucked her against his chest, hugging gently in that big protective way of his that she soaked up like a sponge. "All I know for sure is that both he and I adore you. We will do anything to keep you safe, but more than that we want you to be happy. So as mixed up and confused as my split personality shifter shit is, you can still count on me to be there for you. Either form."

Stephanie twisted her head to rest her cheek on his chest. She slid her arms around his waist and committed fully to the embrace. "Thank you for that. And I'm making this up as I go along, too. You're a good man, Blue. And a good wolf." She reached up briefly and patted his back as if he were still in his wolf form. "We'll figure it out. We'll figure *something* out."

Because there had to be a way to keep all the good things that had been happening in her world going. Winning the lodge, getting to be with her friend and sister full time, finding good new friends. All of that needed to continue, and if she got to have something special for herself—

Nope. That's where the magical fairy tale stalled out for her. Right now she could see no way forward.

"Hey." Strong fingers tucked under her chin and lifted her head until her gaze met the sharp blue eyes of a wolf. "No pressure. Just you and me and the furry guy, and somehow it will be exactly right for us."

"Okay." She let it go at that.

Because you never told the happy people in the fairy tale that disaster was bound to strike.

HEAVEN AND HELL. Such a perfect mix. Time alone with Steph verses time alone with Steph where they could truly enjoy being trapped alone.

The storm continued to rage all afternoon, which meant Blue and Stephanie had to entertain themselves. Unfortunately it didn't mean bouncing hard on the big bed down in the basement until they were dizzy with pleasure.

Instead, they played cards. They read to each other from a riddle book and laughed until their stomachs hurt. They made origami paper boats—Blue knew how—and floated them in the puddles outside the porch overhang. That was not quite as successful because of the wind that whipped overhead, tipping their sailboats over on a regular basis.

By the time evening rolled around, Blue finally felt normal. His wolf was pouting, the best that he could figure, but was no longer snapping or trying to take over.

While Stephanie put together a stir fry, Blue cooked up a salmon steak they'd found in the freezer. He also raided the wine cellar, pulling out a very nice Viognier white to go with their meal.

Sitting at the big, long formal dining table was cozy because of Steph. She found an extra chair and pulled it into the room, placing them kitty-corner to each other. Him behind the table and her at the head, both with great views of the continuing light show outside the window.

"This storm means business, doesn't it?" Steph stared

for a moment, her wine glass caught in mid-air as an exceptionally bright flash raced across the sky. Sparkles danced around the room.

"It's a good one, but I don't think we need to start building an ark. It'll be done by morning, I think."

She sipped her wine and ate another piece of his admittedly excellent salmon. "Not that I wouldn't have asked you this anyway, and not that you haven't been asked some variation of this over the past months by Cassidy, or Stace, or all three of us at once, but..." She made a face.

"What?"

She laid her fork down and folded her hands. "Buddy mate, I need some advice about how to help my family."

"Let's go with buddy or mate, not both. That sounds like a confused sailor," he suggested, still hugely amused. "What specific area do you need to help them with more than you're already doing? Because you are a big help at the lodge and super-important to all of them."

She tilted her head from side to side. "Oh, I get along great with everyone. And I love them dearly, and I know they love me. It's not that."

"Confused mate over here, still."

She met his gaze. "That sounds so..."

"Good?"

"Formal."

"Good and formal."

Steph rolled her eyes. "If I have a question, are you bound by mate law to keep it secret?"

She asked it playfully, but there was a sudden dash of something in her eyes.

His wolf shot to attention. *She's afraid.*

I'm human, not unaware he snapped at his other self even as he fought to keep his expression light. "I think this is another of those times I need to hear the question to know the right answer. I will keep all your secrets that can be kept safely."

She stuck out her tongue. "I wish I'd never trained you to stop being Mr. Cooperative."

A shrug. "I want the best for you, remember? If I'm tied up in secret-keeping, that might mean I don't have the ability to do what needs to be done."

Although he totally got it. There were things in his past that he'd never told a soul about that were going to stay that way for many good reasons.

"Here's the real question. We've got this timeline, and I really want to do my part to make sure we win the challenge."

Blue nodded. "Yes. And your spa is a huge hit for the guests at the lodge, so mission well underway."

"No, I want to do more. I want to make sure this doesn't fall apart because we missed something."

She nibbled on her bottom lip, and Blue focused hard on her eyes to control the tremble of need that shot through his body. This was a serious topic, and he needed to pay it serious attention.

"I'm listening. You want to make sure that the Wilson pack gives you approval and says the lodge is permanently yours."

Still thoughtful, Stephanie nodded. "Up until now we've been really focusing on getting the lodge running and making sure that it's a great place. But what about leaning a little harder to the personal human angle? Or maybe I should say personal wolf angle."

Oh. He thought he knew where she was going with this. "Approach the Wilson pack to see how you're doing?"

"Do we even know any of the Wilson pack?" She leaned forward now, interest running high.

Blue considered. "There is overlap between the Wilson pack and the Jasper pack. It's a little complicated—they're not really two packs. Not like it would be in another town when you mentioned two names like that. The Wilson pack were the original settlers in this area. They've kind of been grandfathered as a side shoot and given an honorary level of respect."

"So, we could have them over?" Her excitement faded suddenly into concern. "But if we do it too soon, it could ruin our chances. Because if we're not completely fantastic, it would set the wrong tone."

"No. Back up a bit, I think you've got something here. There are extended Wilson family members in our pack." Something itched at the back of his brain, and he fought to find it. Happiness bloomed as he realized what it was. "One of those families includes a teenager who will be out at the lodge sometime this coming week."

Stephanie's face lit up. "For the whole teenage *come hang out and be good wolfies* evening. That's fantastic." She considered. "Do you think she'd be picked up or dropped off by a family member who we could chitchat with casually for while?"

His mind raced. "Here's a bit of wolf info you may not know, but it really helps your idea. Because the Wilson pack is considered partly separate from ours, a formal invitation is *required* for a certain level of mixing and matching. It would be completely appropriate to suggest it was okay for one of the more senior Wilson members to ensure their teen is in the right place at the right time."

"And you can do that? I mean, will you do that?"

"It would be my pleasure."

The way she looked at him—with stars in her eyes—Blue wanted that from now to forever.

Plans in place, the rest of the evening vanished into thin air and reading in front of a roaring fire. Blue had zero problems with François's opulent living arrangements.

Bastard just needed to keep his hands off Blue's mate.

It came time to settle down for the night, Blue already had a plan in place. He wanted to dive in one hundred percent, and that kiss had driven his interest even higher. But they had layers to build in this relationship, and after waiting this long, it wasn't going to kill him to wait a little longer.

"Hey, I've got an idea." He leaned against the bathroom door where Stephanie was rumbling in the cupboards to find toothbrushes. When she met his gaze, he handed her a T-shirt from his emergency stash in the Jeep. Knowing she was about to be enveloped in his scent was very satisfying. "Use these for pajamas. I set up a bed for you in front of the fireplace."

Amusement danced in her eyes, but her cheeks flushed slightly. "We're not going to use the big bed down in the dungeon?"

Blue cut off the growl that ripped free. He cleared his throat. "It appears my wolf has opinions about that room. I think you'll be comfy in the alternative location."

He disappeared before she could ask any more questions.

Shifting to his wolf went faster than usual because the beast was eager to be in charge. He all but pranced to the layers of blankets his human side had carefully arranged in front of the fireplace. He laid down in the middle and rolled onto his back, wiggling gently to make sure his scent was all over the sheets.

You are one annoying asshole, Blue told his wolf. He considered and then added honestly, *but I'm absolutely on board this time.*

He shuffled to the side so there was just enough room for Stephanie to stretch out beside him. Then he put his nose down on his paws and waited for her to join him.

9

Stephanie laid her toothbrush on the counter and squared her shoulders. They'd had a wonderful evening together, and now she was tingling from head to toe with anticipation. What exactly was going to be happening tonight was up in the air, but she knew it was going to be good.

The man could kiss. The kiss that she hadn't wanted to stop had kept running through her brain at the most inconvenient moments all evening.

Heart pounding slightly, she walked as confidently as possible into the living room.

A flash of disappointment hit, but then happiness bloomed. If Blue had been stretched out like a smorgasbord, stark naked, she'd have enjoyed it to some degree. But being here in this room with him in his wolf and the flames of the fire dying down to warm, glowing amber was perfect.

She took a running leap, landing with a bounce on the homemade mattress next to Blue's wolf self.

He let out a snort as if amused.

She laid a hand on his head and tightened her grip

slightly. "You're a goof. But I appreciate what you've done here. Thank you." She leaned down and pressed a kiss between his eyes. She didn't back up fast enough, and as she leaned away, he got in an opportunist lick up the side of her cheek. "Dude. I already washed my face."

He eased to the side the smallest amount, tongue hanging out as he offered a wolfy grin.

"Yeah, I know. Wolf germs are good germs or something like that. Don't try it again," she warned sternly.

She settled herself on the layers of blankets that Blue had stacked into a soft nest. He turned and tucked himself into a spot so that he could nestle against her and still look at her.

She stroked the soft fur around his ear. "I need to not think about this too hard or it gets kind of weird, but if I go with the flow and enjoy it, it's amazing. You are one beautiful wolf, Blue."

He sighed softly, closing his eyes contentedly.

Sleep came, despite the crashing storm that continued outside.

Until the comfortable, warm sensation inside shattered, changing into teeth and claws, and Stephanie shivered.

Into her happiness, anger swirled. A dark, nasty sensation, with an unholy pleasure mixed in. Stephanie was looking once again into a pair of dark brown eyes full of malice and lust. A pair of eyes that went from flashing with hate to pain filled and fading, and blood covered her hands.

Stephanie backed away from the body in horror, his arms clutching her feet. Her heart pounded and—

"Stephanie, wake up."

The words were somewhere between gentle and a demand, and even as she shivered, she opened her eyes.

Blue was curled around her, his strong arms wrapped around her shoulders and his face only inches away.

"Blue?"

"It's okay," he assured her, fingers pushing her hair back behind her ear. "You're okay."

"I know that." But even as she said the words, she recalled more. "I was remembering...a nightmare."

He bumped his nose into hers. "You were shivering and then you swore. You said the word *never* very forcefully and started to cry." His arms tightened around her, and now he was petting her back as if he needed to be touching her.

Stephanie was torn between accepting the comfort and being absolutely horrified that he'd witnessed and heard any of that. Maybe the less said the better. Maybe he'd forget about it and not ask more questions.

"Thanks for waking me up."

She reached up to pat his shoulder in a friendly manner when it finally registered.

Blue was naked as a jaybird.

She took a quick look. "Um. Naked."

He shrugged. "You were scared, and my wolf couldn't do much more than lick. I didn't think that was going to be enough, so I shifted."

Talk about a great way to be distracted from bad memories and places her mind didn't want to go. "Naked looks good on you."

Pride bloomed on his face. "I'm glad you think so."

Stroking his skin was a necessity. Fingertips easing along the ridges of muscle, she savored the contrast between silky softness and rock-hard biceps. She smoothed over the firm swoop of his chest muscles then teased her fingertips over his nipples.

"Steph?"

"Hmm?" Yes, as far as distractions went, naked Blue was at the very top of her list.

He laid a hand over hers to stop her exploring caresses. "You should go back to sleep."

"Don't want to sleep," she admitted with full honesty.

A deep shuddering breath lifted his chest. "Shit."

Amusement bubbled up and chased away another layer of the cold memory. "If you're tired, don't worry. You just lay back and imagine you're on a beach or something."

She pressed a hand to his shoulder. No way could she push him over, so he had to have gone willingly to the mattress surface. Which left her with a wonderful playground to explore.

She skimmed a hand down his ribs, tapping her fingers along the Adonis muscle arrowing toward his groin. His erection rose from a neat patch of blond curls. Full and hard and very, very pretty.

Blue met her gaze steadily when she lifted her eyes to examine his face

His nostrils flared when she wrapped her fingers around his length, his expression so serious. Far too serious for a man with a woman's hand wrapped around his cock.

"Yes?" she asked.

"Always. Anytime you want. I'm yours to touch, to take, anything you need."

Stephanie moved her hands slowly upward, savouring the sensation of heat and strength. "I thought we talked about you offering everything without getting clarification."

"This absolutely doesn't need to be clarified," Blue assured her right before his eyes rolled back in his head because she'd adjusted her grip, taking advantage of the moisture already leaking from the head of his cock. Her palm slid over him, heat wrapping around him like an exotic blanket.

So much to see. So much to experience as she touched him for the first time. Intimate, a sexual connection yes, but also one of simply giving pleasure to this man who had been her friend over the last months.

She could have justified that she'd noticed wolves were far more physical creatures. Justified by saying there was nothing wrong with two grown adults enjoying each other's company in a physical way.

But at the deepest core of her, she knew the truth. This didn't need to be justified.

It was her and Blue, and they were right together.

She was glad he didn't try to take over. Didn't try to turn this into an event for both of them, because right now she wanted to give. And as she gave attention to his cock, stroking him smoothly to find all the rhythms that made him moan with happiness, Stephanie felt the connection between them grow stronger.

She leaned in and pressed her lips to his, accepting his eager kiss. His tongue tangled with hers even as she kept the rhythm of her hand in motion. Like being in a dream world, somewhere along the limits of imagination, Stephanie kissed the man who would be her mate. Skimmed the palm of her hand over the head of his cock then increased the speed until he was swearing, curling against her, stomach muscles gone rigid.

He tucked his fingers into the hair at the back of her head and tugged their lips apart far enough to meet her eyes. Then his cock jerked in her hand, moisture shooting between them, and he moaned out her name with pleasure written in every line of his face.

Blue collapsed back onto the mattress, arms flung to the

side, his still heavy cock rising like the leaning tower from his groin. "Wow. Did not see that one coming."

"And I only sort of saw it coming because we were kissing," Stephanie teased.

He twisted his head to meet her gaze and winked. "Thanks. I really enjoyed that."

"Me, too," she shared honestly. A yawn of extraordinary size overtook her. "Oops. Excuse me."

But he nodded, curling up to a sitting position. "Give me a minute to get cleaned up, then we'll try to get some more shut eye."

Which is the first time Stephanie had noticed. "The storm. I can't hear it anymore."

"Good. It still might be tough to get out of here tomorrow, but there might be a way." He kissed her briefly before rising to his feet and sauntering out of the room with a satisfied air.

Stephanie followed, washing her hands in the kitchen sink. She beat him back to the mattress and rearranged things a little bit, placing an extra pillow to the side of the one she'd been using.

When he returned, she patted the space next to her. "You don't have to shift. Like you said, let's try and get a little more rest."

And even after that lovely distraction, it was good to have one more thing to tip her over the edge into sleep. Blue settled beside her then snuggled her against him. Spooning her body in close and wrapping her up in a tight Hug. Not possessive, not protective. Just together.

Just perfect.

❧

SHE WAS AMAZING. Blue had always seen Stephanie as an optimistic person and someone he could trust, and now he had more confirmation of her heart of gold.

There had been no deceit in her when she gave to him so willingly the night before. It wasn't as if she said she wanted to touch him and then expected him to get her off in return.

Although he was totally going to return the favour. Craved the chance, in fact. Bringing her to a screaming orgasm a dozen times over might be enough to start evening the score, but as Blue stared down at her the next morning, he soaked in the satisfaction warming his core.

She'd touched him. Trusted him. Now she still slept like the innocent she was and knew he'd be there for her.

Or at least that's what he hoped was going on in her head and heart.

It was as good a start as he could have hoped for. But that's what it was—a start.

Blue laid there to enjoy a few more minutes of holding his mate in his arms, but he made sure to get up before she stirred. He took a look around outside, wandering down the road to see exactly how big a mess they were facing. While everything was soaked, the winds had picked up enough to improve how well everything was drying out.

So he made some decisions and loaded up the pictures into the Jeep, planning to get him and Stephanie out of there before another flash storm got them stuck.

Although sometime in the future he totally wanted to be trapped with his mate for an extended period of time.

He'd just finished loading the Jeep when Stephanie stumbled into the kitchen, all soft and sleep ruffled. His shirt hung to mid-thigh, and her hair hung tossed around her shoulders. She'd been scratching her fingers through it.

"Hey, Blue. What's new?"

God, she looked adorable. "I think we can get off the mountain. But there's no rush," he hurried to assure her when she straightened and blinked rapidly. "Another hour to let the sun hit the road and for the wind to do its job could be helpful. If you want to grab a shower, go for it."

She nodded but paused, looking up at him with smoky eyes. "Are you going to have a shower too?"

Dear God in heaven. Temptation being offered to him on a silver platter. Blue swallowed hard but stuck to his guns.

Somehow he managed to shake his head instead of nod vigorously. "You go ahead by yourself this time."

A flash of disappointment but also relief danced over her face, and Blue knew he'd made the right choice.

She lifted her chin and offered a sweet smile. "Another time?"

Blue stepped closer and gathered her in his arms, giving her the truth. "Absolutely. We'll stay in the shower until we're all wrinkly and pruney and can't stand because we've had so much fun touching each other."

She swallowed visibly then nodded her head rapidly. "Okay. That sounds like a plan."

She tilted her head back, pressed a kiss to his jaw, then slipped from his arms. She wiggled her fingers goodbye and escaped to the bathroom.

Blue walked outside and breathed deeply for a while, thinking about gas mileage equations to try to get his hard-on to go away.

Getting down the mountain required all his concentration. Stephanie white-knuckled it for the first while then seemed to relax into her seat. She was still bouncing rapidly, but the level of trust she showed in his driving was enough to make him want to preen. They both were quiet for the trip back to the lodge, just sharing the occasional glance at each other and a secretive smile.

Once they reached the main highway, Blue grabbed her hand. He squeezed her fingers lightly, just because he needed to touch her.

Pulling in as close to the front door of Timberwolf Lodge as possible, Blue turned off the Jeep and turned to face her. "You ready for this?"

She flashed a grin, but it was wobbly at the edges. "I'm always ready for this." She paused, and an enormous sigh escaped her.

"*Stephanie*," he warned. "This is me. Your friend, first and foremost. Don't lie to me."

"Okay, I'm a little nervous," she admitted. "My friends are going to be ecstatic when they hear the news about us being practice mates, because they've bought into the whole *wolfies are the best*. And I'm not saying that you aren't, but we're trying to go slow, remember?"

"I remember."

"So how do we make this thing between us stay slow when Tweedledee and Tweedledum and their mates will probably start planning a celebration?"

Blue shrugged. "We tell our friends we're going slow. They're not assholes." He considered. "Okay. Jace is an asshole some of the time, but he'll still listen to us if we say something."

"Ugh. We have to talk, and use words, and everything?"

"I know. How rude."

This time when they smiled at each other, the amusement in her eyes was real.

"I got it. We'll tell them we're M-I-Ts." He winked. "Mates in training."

A solid snort escaped her, and she lifted a hand and covered her nose. "Stacy will ask which of us is the right mitt and which the left."

"Del will make some crack about us having matching toques."

"Cassidy will try to come up with an acronym for *toque* that's dirty."

They were so focused on each other that a knock on the window beside Blue's head nearly had him levitating out of his seat.

He whirled in place to discover Marvin the moose had pressed his big nose to the pane, wide rack looming overhead. "Hey, back up, buster."

The moose shrugged then lazily turned away, sauntering down the road toward the trees.

"And I guess that's our cue that it's time for the next thing." Stephanie was the one to reach for his hand. "Blue, just so you know, nothing is set in stone right now, and nothing is simple. But this part I can say; I like you, and I want to be with you as much as it works."

Which wasn't a full-on *bite me, mark me, make me yours* declaration, but for now?

It was enough.

10

Stephanie climbed up into the back of the Jeep. Blue had barely managed to untie the load of artwork when the horde descended.

Jace was in the middle of reaching for the first painting Stephanie held out to him when he froze. His gaze swung between Steph and Blue, then his face broke into an enormous grin. "Blue? Is there something you'd like to share with the rest of the class?"

Everyone who was gathered paused.

Del sniffed deep, and he too grinned like a banshee.

Before Blue could say anything, though, Steph took charge. "All of you with magic sniffers can just stop right now. It's very rude to not include everyone in the conversation." She stepped to the side of the Jeep and raised her chin. "Everyone. Listen up."

She thrust a hand toward Blue.

Instinctively, he took it, tangling their fingers together, holding hands in a lopsided position with one in and one out of the Jeep.

Even as smiles began to grow, Stephanie tilted her head

to an even more regal angle. "Blue and I are involved. We are not yet mates, we are mates in training. While we figure out exactly how this relationship will work, please keep your sniffing to yourself and let's get on with our task at hand."

Cassidy pressed her fists to the top of her hips. "Well, that's just mean. Exciting news, and we're not allowed to get excited about it?"

"I agree," Stacy said. Her eyes sparkled, and for a moment she pressed her hands to her chest and offered an adoring big-sister smile to Stephanie. "So, you guys are *mitts*. Who's the left and who's the right?"

"I want to know what colour matching toques to get them." Del held out a hand to Blue. "I know, I know. Nothing is official, but I still need to say congrats."

Blue was outright laughing as he glanced over at Steph. "Two out of three so far."

"Give it time." She clapped her hands together. "Remember that part about getting on with our task at hand?"

Somehow it was enough to get them all moving in different directions. Which meant once the canvases had been transferred from the back of the Jeep to leaning against the wall in the massive dining hall, Blue was shanghaied and hauled outside by Jace and Del.

Jace pushed him to a sitting position beside the fire pit, both hands resting on Blue's shoulders. His alpha had a strange expression on his face. "You can't do anything the easy way, can you?"

"Seems not." Now that the guys we're alone, it was safe to open another conversation. "Yes, it sucks that Stephanie hasn't just up and accepted me as her mate. But I am thrilled that she's not freaking out or outright saying no. So really, things are pretty good right now. Couple of issues, though. The painter dude? He's absolutely on my shit list."

Del frowned, settling in the chair next to him. "I thought you said he wasn't even at the cabin."

It took a couple minutes to explain the whole painting fiasco, along with the potential stalking and his wolf's severe dislike of François.

At the end of it, Jace nodded. "I agree with Stephanie. If she's okay with the pictures being in the lodge, we'll keep them. But we are definitely having a conversation with this cougar to tell him to mind his manners."

Blue moved on to the other important matter at hand. "Stephanie had a great idea in terms of moving toward the goal of ensuring the girls could keep Timberwolf Lodge. Are you okay with me getting in touch with the Wilson family?"

It was Del's turn to make a face. "The ladies are nowhere near ready to win the challenge."

"But a little bit of relationship building might grease the wheels," Blue pointed out.

Jace considered for a moment then nodded. "You know who'd be best to get in touch with. Did you have something specific in mind?"

"The teen event on Thursday." Blue pointed at Del. "Stacy being pack mom to everyone might work in our favour. The youngest Wilson will be attending."

Understanding shot to high. "Carolyn Wilson. She's a good kid."

"She is. Unlike others in the family." Like the banished Emma.

Before Blue could bring up that issue, he spotted a quick flash of light in the nearby trees. Once. Twice. Once.

Damn. That had been quick. Which meant a different

matter had to be addressed immediately. "Heads up. We're getting a visit from one of my army buddies," Blue informed his friends.

The other two men exchanged a glance. "You mean we actually get to meet somebody from the mythical Shifter Special Forces?" Del drawled.

"Be nice to him, or he'll have to kill you," Blue deadpanned in answer.

He didn't often talk about his time in the military. It had been another one of those things his Omega side had led him into. He'd gone along for the ride because there were times it was just not worth arguing with the beast.

Some of what had happened during that time had not been very pretty, but Blue had made some good friends.

"So, when?" Jace asked. "Next week?"

"Thirty seconds from now. If that's okay with you."

His friend stared at him hard. "You're not really asking for permission, are you?" Jace offered in a long-suffering tone.

Blue glanced toward the sky as if considering. "Nope."

"Pretty much situation normal, then," Del interjected. He'd twisted toward the trees and was watching intently as Lance Colburn marched toward them across the green lawn of Timberwolf Lodge.

His hair was still cut in a short military style. The rest of his physique had, if anything, gotten leaner and fitter. The man had always been a lethal weapon, but in the couple of years since Blue had last seen him, he had grown even more taut.

Blue closed the distance between them and held a hand toward his friend. "Lance, my man. Thanks for coming."

Lance used the grasp to haul him in tight and proceeded to bang a couple of ribs out of place with his enthusiastic back pat. "My brother asked for help, so I'm here. You know how this works."

Blue winked. "Kind of hoped it wasn't only out of obligation."

Another firm pat, this time to his shoulder, nearly sent Blue sprawling to the ground. The two glanced at each other and laughed.

"Behave," Blue ordered with mock annoyance. "I'm supposed to introduce you to my Alpha, and here you are acting like a jackass."

Lance had already turned to Jace. Dark black eyes met Jace's blue ones, and the two men assessed each other. Power rippled on the surface of the air, which was typical when powerful wolves met, but not a thing that had to happen right now. Not if Blue's ideas for Lance's time at Timberwolf Lodge were to be of any positive effect.

He sauntered forward and nudged Lance out of the way en route to a central position between the two men. "Without actually hauling your dicks out, do you think you can pull the dominance discussion into check for a moment? Jace, this is my buddy, Lance Colburn. Lance, Jace Carter, my cousin and the newest Alpha of the Jasper pack."

Lance let his shoulders fall into a relaxed position. Reaching forward as if he were no more than a human, he offered his hand. "Good to meet you. Permission to come onto your lands, sir?"

"Permission granted," Jace said formally. He tilted his head toward Del. "Pack Enforcer. Also a Carter on his mom's side."

Del joined the mix, shaking Lance's hand then stepping back and folding his arms over his chest. "Delaney. But you can call me Del."

Lance eyed the three of them. "Jeez, Blue. I'm at a fucking Carter family reunion."

"Just you wait. There's a whole bunch more of us hiding in the trees."

Lance rested his hands behind his back, standing at ease in the position that said he was still a half second away from being able to rip out someone's throat. "Happy to report there's no one in these trees. Not at the moment. But if you want more information about the other matter we discussed, we should talk."

Blue guided them back to the firepit. He pulled open the fake rock door that covered the beer cooler he and Steph had hidden a few weeks ago. "Make yourself comfortable, because this is the group you need to share your intel with." He passed everyone a beer, grinning at Del's shocked expression. "What? You never sniffed out my stash?"

"You are such an ass," Del offered lightly.

"Tsk, tsk, tsk," Blue warned. "Just remember all those young teenage minds that will be trotting around here in a few days. Your mate would not be happy to hear you speak in such a way."

Del gave him a look. "Oh, and what would your mate-in-training say about you hiding alcohol out here where anyone can get at it? Including those young impressionable teenagers?"

Blue flicked the top off his beer, caught the lid in mid-air, then tucked it neatly in to his pocket. "My mate-in-training would be the co-conspirator who helped hide the cooler here. Plus, there's a code system. So be nice to me, or I won't tell you how to get refreshments.

Jace rolled his eyes. "Is this a component of your Omega-ness?"

"The fact that I have really great taste in alcoholic beverages?"

"The fact you can't do anything without trying to piss off at least one person."

"I think it has less to do with me being an Omega and more to do with me just being me," Blue said honestly.

He met gazes with his friend. "You look as if you just stumbled onto a vaudeville routine."

"You three are damn entertaining," Lance commented, sipping his beer. "Mate-in-training?"

"It's a long story," Blue offered with a wave of his hand. "Details I'll share later. What did you find out about Dwight, our missing human who is possibly a blackmailer... or worse."

The tension in the group rose, all nonchalance and laziness vanishing.

"Toronto said he vanished without a clue," Del offered softly.

Lance shrugged. "To the average tracker, I suppose. I'm not average. There were plenty of signs. The man was not even trying to be sneaky after a certain point. He's headed this way." He looked directly at Jace. "Blue called me in, but since you're the Alpha, I need to know what your orders are. You want me to follow him? Is he a direct threat?"

"We don't know," Jace said honestly. "Is he actually in Jasper?"

Lance shook his head. "He's booked an Airbnb, though, so we'll know where he is once he arrives."

Del spoke up. "Jace you have every right as ruling Alpha to have a through discussion with any wolf who trespasses on your territory."

"Not a wolf," Blue reminded Del.

"Well, us being the biggest baddies in the area says we

can still have a talk with the man, wolf or not." Del eyed Lance with curiosity. "Good job tracking."

Lance dipped his chin a fraction of an inch. "It's my job."

"In the meantime, we're going to give you a slightly different job," Jace said. "We've got to explain having a new dominant in the area, and an old friend visiting Blue works. You have my official permission to remain in the territory, and we'll set you up in one of the cabins here. I'll have you pull some security shifts here around the lodge, not only to keep an eye out for Dwight, but for a certain cougar who needs to learn to behave before he becomes a very pretty rug for my living room."

Interest rose in Lance's eyes. "Oh, now this sounds like a story I need to hear."

It felt good to be gathered there with his friends, but part of what made it even better for Blue was knowing that Stephanie was also being thoroughly grilled by her sister and friend. And the only result from that would be positive in Blue's favour.

He had a whole team on his side, and it was an amazing feeling.

THE INSTANT the guys took off outside, Cassidy snapped a finger and pointed upstairs. "To the Batcave," she ordered.

Then she marched up the stairs with her back to Stephanie, which meant there was nothing to do except follow.

So she followed and offered a mumbled complaint to her sister. "This is not getting the paintings hung all over the lodge."

"Give it a rest," Stacy snapped with less amusement in her tone than Stephanie had expected.

She glanced over her shoulder at her sister. "Who put a bee in your butt?"

Stacy did a reenactment of Cassidy and pointed forward like a bloodhound. "Move your ass."

Two minutes later they were settled in their unofficial clubhouse, aka, Stacy's wonderous balcony, with comfy seating for each of them which they had personalized with throw cushions and pillows that fit perfectly.

The third degree was about to happen.

She wished in some ways that she could skip some of it. There were too many unanswered questions for her own comfort, but that wasn't what made her hesitate.

She and Blue—

Just the thought of it made something inside of her warm. She wanted to hold onto that brand-new sensation as long as she could. Not analyze and subdivide it. Possibly tarnish it.

Now the problem was telling her two besties something to that effect, and while she wasn't considered a wordsmith by any means, she usually had some idea of how to get the gist across.

She accepted the cup of tea her sister handed her. With her fingers wrapped around the bowl, she enjoyed the heat pressing into her palms. She was still thinking of how to open the conversation, pretty sure one of the two of them would get a word in before she'd finalized her thoughts. But wonder of wonders, her sister and best friend sat in silence, the two of them breathing deeply and staring out over the scenery.

Which was odd and meant she had no choice. Her tongue started without her.

"I can't tell if this is some kind of trick you're playing," Stephanie complained. "Like, I know, instead of pelting Stephanie with all sorts of questions, we're going to sit here without speaking until she up and confesses every single little thing that's on her mind."

A soft laugh drifted from Cassidy. "Is it working?"

"No," Stephanie said primly. "I have no desire to tell you that I'm shocked and astonished and somehow humbled that Blue says we're mates. Fuck my life."

Stacy laughed as she laid a hand on Steph's arm. "I like that you're so quiet and laid back. Never a peep out of you."

"And ladylike. Don't forget that," Cassidy murmured with amusement.

The worry that had built faded. They were her family. Her forever and ever family, and they would understand.

"I'm excited, but I'm scared. And I'm telling the truth when I say I'm not sure what I want right now. But I know how special having a mate is, and I know how special Blue is, so I'm not going to do anything to hurt him, or me, or us. I just need time."

Cassidy's gaze drifted off the landscape and onto her, and as their eyes met, there was something new in the depths. Something unexpected because—although not a wolf herself—it had wolf-like leanings to it.

"I think I know what you mean. You are special, Steph, and we love you very much. Considering how you think about people, and how deep relationship connections work for you, I get that this might take time." Cass wrinkled her nose. "The hard part is the *not wanting to hurt anybody*. If you don't accept Blue as a mate, it's going to devastate him, and there's nothing you can do to change that."

Which she knew to the core of her being but couldn't explain. Couldn't share the one huge reason there could be no final connection between her and Blue. "If he was in my life from now to forever, I would not be unhappy about that," Stephanie said.

"But in your life forever as a friend or as a mate?" Stacy asked. "Because, sweetie, having dated Del for a short period of time, it's not remotely the same thing. There's a depth to being mates that's beyond human imagining. The connection between us is astonishing."

Which made Steph's back stiffen and her resolve grow iron strong. There would be *no* connection like that between her and Blue.

But she smiled and did her best to put on a good front for the girls. "For now, let's not worry about things that far in advance. I've got something else to tell you, both good and bad."

It felt right to change the topic away from her and Blue. Moving briefly over the fact that she had an unwanted admirer in their artist de jour then to her idea for starting to make inroads with the Wilson pack.

Stacy outright grinned at the idea of sweet-talking the Wilsons when Carolyn was visiting on Thursday. "The teens really are good kids." She bumped her foot into Cassidy's when the other woman snorted. "Please. You know what it was like when we had hormones to deal with as humans. Add in all the shifter nonsense, and I think our pack is doing extraordinarily well."

Cassidy peered over the top of her teacup at Stacy. "Jordan Freshet *peed* on Gaia's leg. In the middle of the street. That's not typical teenage behavior."

"Teenage *wolf* behavior. Not approved, but understandable," Stacy offered primly. "Territory marking is a big impulse amongst the males."

Cassidy folded her arms over her chest. "If Jace ever

tried to pee on me, the man would squat for the rest of his life."

Stephanie thought back to the slash marks on the painting and decided to hold her tongue. It hadn't upset her. The claws? A little, yes, but not the territory marking.

Right about then, action started down in the yard. The guys had gathered by the firepit, their equivalent of the balcony. But now another figure appeared out of the trees and marched to join them.

Stephanie, Stacy, and Cassidy all watched in interest as a bit of back pounding took place.

"Any idea what's going on?"

Cassidy considered for a minute, obviously discussing something with Jace though the *woo-woo* connection they had. "Friend of Blue's, military. He comes in peace, and I think he's going to be a good help. Jace is happy."

Good enough for Steph. It was time for the next thing. She clapped her hands and shot to her feet. "Now. We have twelve paintings that are absolutely amazing, and we need to figure out the best places to put them. Can we get to work?"

The other women exchanged a glance then thrust their hands into the middle to connect with Steph's at-the-ready fist.

"Bibbity," said Cassidy.

"Bobbity," Stephanie offered happily because her friends being there for her all the time was perfect. But there was such a thing as too much togetherness when it came down to it.

Stacy eyed her as if she'd overheard that last mental thought. Then she shook her head and finished the ritual. "Boom."

Then she raised a finger and shook it in Steph's face.

"You are going to date that man officially. And you are going to treat him nice, and I'm not talking about sex."

"But she's totally talking about sex," Cassidy offered dryly.

"Enough with the advice," Stephanie said. "I'm a big girl. I can take care of my guy."

Her guy. That didn't sound too bad.

And then Cassidy offered up the perfect conclusion. She grinned. "Mitts and toques. And by toques, I mean *Taking Off Clothes, Uninhibited Excitement.*"

Stacy rolled her eyes. "Toque is not spelled with a C. It's a Q."

Stephanie didn't care. She grabbed the railing and whistled sharply. Four pairs of eyes focused their direction. She waved hard at Blue and shouted down at him, "Three out of three. We win."

When Blue raised an arm in the air and flashed her a thumbs-up, that warm glow inside flared brighter.

This was going to be a big new adventure.

11

Preparation for the youth event took over Blue's life. What he wanted to do was curl up with his mate. Spending half the time getting hot and heavy, and half the time just cuddling and sharing intimate stories.

What he got instead was a to-do list as long as his arm and a whole lot of people ordering him around.

Which was not an activity that Blue enjoyed very much, because, as he realized with a rush, he normally ignored orders, what with being an Omega and all.

But when Stephanie took off with the lodge SUV for a run to Costco with an enormous grocery list—the drive alone taking over two hours—he meekly accepted the checklist Cassidy handed him.

"You can just take that evil glint out of your eyes," he informed her primly. "I know what you're doing."

She raised a brow, and suddenly he was looking at a mirror image to the expression Jace used when *he* was being high and mighty Alpha.

Blue had to point out a few things. "You do know that

ordering me around with your magic Alpha voice probably won't work."

"You poor deceived child. It's not my Alpha voice that I'll be using. It's my *I'm besties with your mate-in-training, and if you want this relationship to work out, you're going to be nice to me* voice." She patted him on the cheek. "Now, be a good lad and get Lance to help you. According to the real boss of this event, Stacy says they need lots of physical activities planned to keep the teens' energy levels in check."

Blue whipped off as irrelevant of a salute as possible. "Yes, ma'am."

He sauntered into the yard, whistling.

Lance and Del were placing a pop-up tent over the future refreshment table.

"You're with me, buddy," Blue shouted at his friend. "We're setting up a scavenger hunt."

Lance raised a brow. "Why don't we take them hunting?"

Unbidden laughter escaped from Del. He worked hard to control his expression but with little luck. "That will be another time down the road. My mate, although aware that we're predators, is currently worried about the local bunny population."

Lance snorted. "You're kidding."

Del shook his head, glancing toward the house to be sure there were no humans within earshot. "I suggested the gardens she's growing would be safer with fewer hopping scroungers around, but she's got some sweet *bunnies are pets* image going on in her head." He shrugged. "It's so adorable I can't bring myself to destroy her illusions."

Five minutes later, Blue and Lance were wandering through the forest, hiding small bags of candy and beef jerky.

"I've got to say it. You guys all having human mates is just weird."

"Mates are not weird." Blue bristled then considered. "There is a bit of culture gap we're still working on. It's not as if we set out to choose something out of the norm."

Lance took a running start and made it halfway up a tree trunk before propelling himself into midair. He caught a branch and hung suspended a good twenty feet off the ground. He spoke while he tied a bag one-handed far above the height where Blue expected teens to discover it. "I don't know if I'll ever find my mate, given that there's no guarantee. But I want a mate with some teeth."

He dropped to his feet and wiped his hands, glancing up and nodding with satisfaction.

"Teeth are almost always a good choice," Blue teased.

Lance gave him the bird then explained. "You know, a nice brawny babe who can go for hours. Someone who can take on all comers and kick ass."

Blue folded his arms over his chest. "A, you're dreaming. That is not the kind of woman you want or need. And B, you don't a get a choice. It's *mating*. Fated means no choice."

Lance raised a brow. "Maybe I'm a smarter wolf than you. No fragile little human for me. No submissive, either. I'm going to have a wolf who will mind her p's and q's, and I'm going to be the boss, and she will adore me. And that's probably why it'll never happen."

"You want her to be a warrior *and* you expect her to let you boss her around? You're not dreaming, you're hallucinating."

Lance snickered. "The last part was BS. Who would want a yes-man as a mate? I want backbone. Through and through."

A sudden flash of knowledge rushed over Blue. He'd had fewer premonitions in the past months than usual, but this one was strong and bright. His friend with an awestruck expression on his face as his hands reached out to touch the face of a woman.

It was a split second of insight, blurring before the woman's features became clear, but it was enough that Blue grinned.

"Sorry to tell that you that the odds of getting the warrior woman are nil, and you definitely have a mate out there somewhere. She's going to find you, and when she does?" Blue smacked his hands together like smearing a bug on the pavement. "You're not going to know what hit you."

All traces of joking left Lance's face. "Did you just…"

"Uh-huh."

Lance swore and made a face. "Well, um, yay?"

Blue slapped a hand on his friend's back. "Trust me. From one wolf to another who doesn't have what he thought he'd get, we'll muddle through somehow. They're *supposed* to be the perfect one for us. Which at some point means it's going to be perfect. Right?"

Lance offered a long-suffering sigh. "Yay. Woop. Woowhee." Said as if offering a death dirge.

After setting up the scavenger hunt, there was more work to be done. Blue wasn't sure why scrubbing the dock was included in the list of chores—it wasn't as if the teenage wolves would give a shit if it was squeaky clean— but he knew better than to argue with the ladies of the manor.

Steph was still off gathering groceries, so Blue spent the day at Cassidy's beck and call. He took a few breaks to make phones calls and contacts as needed and ended up with astonishing news.

News that he didn't get to share until the morning of the teen event.

Everyone was supposed to start gathering at ten a.m. It should have made for a nice leisurely start to the day, but instead, things were in a semi-panic.

"I hate having Sophie gone," Stacy complained as she and Jessica worked frantically in the kitchen. Breakfast had been late as they were distracted creating the masses of food required to feed the teens all day.

"Where is she?" Stephanie asked as she efficiently made ham sandwiches, one after the other.

"She went to visit a friend on the coast. She hasn't had a holiday since I hired her, so giving her time off was only right. It's just the timing."

"She'll be back tomorrow," Jessica assured her. "In the meantime, I don't mind staying longer to help out," the second assistant chef offered.

Blue took himself outside because the combined scent of Steph and the food being prepared were far too much temptation to put up with.

The teens arrived in small clumps, some before ten, but most in the few minutes after the top of the hour. A few emerged from the trees, dropping small bags from their jaws then shifting and dressing, eager smiles on their faces as they slipped up to greet Jace and Cassidy.

Del and Blue waited by the parking area, greeting those who arrived in their human forms. Del was busy with a group of brothers they'd spent time with the previous month while helping one of them regain control of his wolf after a chemical exposure.

Which left Blue standing alone when a luxury vehicle pulled to a stop beside him.

He'd expected a chauffeur, but it was the grand dame

herself who rose from behind the wheel while Carolyn popped out from the passenger side, vibrating on the spot. She bounced over to Blue, who was doing his best to be polite in two directions.

"Hi Blue, is Stacy here? Have you seen Veronica and Gaia?" Carolyn stopped short as if remembering something. She twisted to present the senior woman walking toward them. "I know you know her, but I'm supposed to do this anyway, right?"

Blue winked. "Yup."

The girl straightened her shoulders and held out a hand that her grandmother graciously took as she closed the final steps to where Blue stood. "Ermeline Wilson, I'd like you to meet Blue Carter, Jasper pack Omega. Blue, this is my grandmother, Ermeline Wilson, matriarch of the Wilson pack and previous Alpha, retired. Revered for her unification of the mountain clans during the battle of Jasper." She leaned toward her grandmother. "Shoot, I was supposed to do that the other way around, wasn't I? Introduce you first?"

Ermeline tilted her head the slightest bit. "Protocol is a hard thing and there will be a time when you must get it exactly right. But Blue and I are old friends, so it's just fine."

The tension eased out of Carolyn's shoulders. "Plus, he's an Omega. He's a good guy, and he doesn't really care about protocol, do you Blue?"

There was a tangled question. Considering this woman held a position of power over Stephanie's future, saying *fuck protocol* as he'd normally do might not be wise.

He went for diplomacy. "I personally try to find a place within the pack where I'm doing what's best for everyone, but I'm also a firm supporter of the hierarchy." The entire time he spoke, he kept eye contact with

Ermeline. "Ma'am, thank you for bringing your granddaughter. We'll make sure she's returned to you happy and well fed."

Ermeline raised a brow regally. "The well fed, you can do. The happy is her choice, isn't it?"

Tangling with ex-Alphas was always a wonderful experience. "We'll do our best not to make her unhappy, then. Is that better?"

She snorted. "Silver-tongued devils, the lot of you."

"Jasper pack?" Blue asked. "Carters?"

"Omegas." Ermeline clarified. She pulled her granddaughter to her side and pressed a kiss to her temple. "Run along, dear, and have fun. Either I or your grandfather will return to pick you up tonight. If that's all right for a different family member to come to the Jasper pack grounds."

"Your family is all welcome," Blue offered quickly.

Carolyn scuffed the ground. "I'd like to run home. Please?"

"Child. You know what your father said."

Carolyn gripped her grandmother's arm. "But you're *his* alpha, so if you say I can run home..."

"Carolyn Wilson," Ermeline admonished. "You do not play those kind of games. You hear me?"

The girl lowered her head, properly chastised because it was a big *no no* to go over your Alpha's head, who in this case, at home, would be her parents.

But Blue remembered those days of wanting to be more independent and spend as much time as possible with his friends.

He cleared his throat. "Perhaps there's a solution that doesn't involve breaking a promise Carolyn has already given to her father." He met Ermeline's gaze. "Would an escort from the Jasper pack Omega and his military-trained friend be sufficient protection for your granddaughter?"

Ermeline considered then dipped her head. She turned to Carolyn, tucked her fingers under her chin, and lifted until their eyes met. "You shouldn't have this privilege after trying to pull a fast one, but I know what it's like to be young, in spite of currently being older than dirt." She glanced at Blue as if assessing him. "You will listen to Blue and his friend, and you will take advantage of the opportunity to not only run but experience the night. Use your senses. Listen and learn. I'll expect a full report the next time we speak. Understand?"

Carolyn looked as if she'd been handed a birthday present wrapped up in a Christmas present rather than a school assignment being tacked onto a fun event. "Thank you, Grandmother, and I will. And I'll tell Dad about all the things I learn too, and I'll be really good, and I love you."

She threw her arms around her grandmother's neck and squeezed tight.

Ermeline allowed it for a moment, then brushed herself off and pulled to an erect position, prim and proper again once Carolyn finally let go. "Enough, I have things to do. Mr. Carter, I leave my granddaughter in your hands. Please ensure you do take good care of her."

"Of course."

She glanced around at Timberwolf Lodge, sniffing lightly. "It seems you have many challenges that you're helping control these days. I wonder if you're up for them all."

She twirled on her heel before Blue could ask for clarification.

Blue watched until her car disappeared up the road before returning to the event.

The meeting seemed to have gone well, but crusty old Alphas had learned a trick or two. Right now, the only sense Blue could get from the experience was that something ominous loomed in the future. A sense of heaviness and danger. Something out of the norm had happened.

He wandered toward the festivities with a heavier heart than expected.

THE ENTIRE AFTERNOON had been filled with memorable moments. Stephanie's stomach still hurt from laughing so hard when a group of teens had accidentally fallen off the dock—no harm done—and the ensuing cannonball contest had grown to include most of the gathered pack.

Then there were the races that had morphed out of a simple challenge between two young males. The next thing they all knew, wolves in either animal or human form were running hellbent for leather around strategically arranged lawn chairs out on the lawn.

Stacy stood beside her youngest son, who bounced up and down next to them as they appreciated the entertainment. "It's like a steeple chase with wolves, isn't it?" she said.

Ace tugged on his mom's leg. "Can I run too?"

Stephanie scooped her nephew up in her arms. "You and I can go for a run later, okay, buddy? We'll let the big kids do this one for now." When his face twisted in disappointment, she motioned for him to lean closer. "I have a secret to tell you."

He leaned in, hand cupped to his ear. "Tell me, Auntie Steph."

Stephanie lowered her voice and said it as mysteriously

as possible. "I bought all the fixings for s'mores *and* banana boats."

His squeal of delight nearly deafened her, and he wiggled to be let down, once again bouncing with hands clasped together. "I want three banana boats. Can I have three, can I?"

Stacy looked concerned before pretending to consider her son's request seriously. "We'll start with one. We should make sure that everybody who wants one can have one, right?"

He nodded seriously then glanced around until he spotted his nanny. The moose shifter was sprawled in an easy chair with a few of the pack's teen boys sitting beside him, listening to him tell a story. "Is it okay if I tell the secret to Marvin?"

"He's the best one to tell. I hear he's a good boat builder," Stacy informed him before twisting his shoulders and giving him a pat on the back. "Go get him, tiger."

She waited until her son was far enough away before she turned and placed her hands on her hips again. "Banana boats? That kid is going to be bouncing for the next week."

"I know. I'm the bestest auntie, aren't I?" Stephanie ducked as her sister gave a halfhearted swing in her direction. Thank goodness for real distractions. "Oops. I see trouble."

She pointed to where one very bushy red wolf was sneaking up on a group of girls suntanning by the lake shore.

Stacy swore. "If that boy pees on my lawn on more time... And poor Gaia. She needs to smack him a good one."

Stephanie grabbed the placemat beside her and rolled it up into a tube. "It's not a newspaper, but it'll work just as well on his nose."

"Or somewhere else. Thanks." Stacy grabbed the roll from Steph's hand and took off at a run to prevent yet another territory marking incident.

There was no way to stop the amusement bubbling inside her. Stephanie had to admit it. She *liked* the wolves. She liked their differences and their quirks. Their enthusiasm and their loyalty.

A warm buzz followed her for the rest of the afternoon.

The sweetest part of the day, though, was after the food had been consumed, and the whole lot of lazy, contented wolves sprawled around the firepit as one of the Carter family played guitar and everyone sang along. Some in wolf, some human. Mostly in key.

Stephanie snuggled under Blue's arm a little tighter where he'd pulled her against him. The soft blanket she'd snagged for them kept the evening cool from drifting below, but his sheer body temperature would have been enough to chase away the cool night air.

Blue linked their fingers together. "Have a good day?"

"I think it went well," she offered.

He nuzzled his lips against her temple. "I agree, but that wasn't my question. How are *you* doing, Stephanie?"

Soft music drifted around them, accompanied by the occasional wavering howl of a wolf. A group of teens giggled on one side of the fire, quieting slightly when Jace offered a glance. Contentment rose from the whole group. Stephanie swore she felt it.

She twisted until she met Blue's gaze. "My family is happy. I'm doing wonderfully."

A small flush of concern was gone from his face before she could really say it had been there. Then he dipped his chin and curled her against him even tighter. "If you're good, then I'm good."

She was going to call him on it. Her being happy didn't mean that he was, then she realized she'd done the same thing. Her happiness was always tied to her family's.

No answer was probably the best answer in this case. The moment was too precious and fragile to destruct with deep, soul-searching ideas.

Stephanie leaned against him and enjoyed the moment.

<h1 style="text-align:center">12</h1>

The run back to Carolyn's home was anticlimactic.

Having to leave Stephanie's side sucked, but Blue found it was tough to stay disappointed considering how eager Carolyn was, paying attention to every move that he and Lance made. After dropping her off and accepting a quick farewell hug, Blue decided to run off a little of his frustration.

He and Lance stretched their legs and ran.

They had worked together before during operations, so this was a flashback to a more organized time in his life with a whole lot of different stress than what came after. It was good to be challenged as Lance nipped at his tail then darted around the corner, skimming over a rocky surface that crumbled apart when Blue moved too slowly.

The chase was on, and he moved with intent. Pulling in strength to draw even with his friend, sneaking around the corner where he knew there was a shortcut, and coming out on top as they rounded the final hill back to home territory.

Blue appreciated the time together and the chance to stretch his legs as a wolf. That sense of incompleteness hovered, but he refused to dwell on the fact that Stephanie was content remaining as they were. It had only been a few days, he reminded his other side.

She's ready his wolf insisted. *She knows it's right.*

Not much use in arguing with the beast when what Blue wanted most of all was for it to be true.

He ducked around the corner of the playhouse and slowed to a stop. Shifting quietly, he waited for Lance to join him.

"Good run," he offered.

Lance took a deep breath. "Fantastic place you've got here. I might have to stick around."

Another one of those flashes of insight struck, and Blue found himself highly amused. "Oh, I don't think that's going to be a problem. For either Jace or your mate."

Lance snapped his attention on him quickly, a touch of annoyance in his eyes. "Stop that."

Blue grinned.

He clapped Lance on the shoulder then tilted his head toward the cabin where he'd been staying. "I'm going to get some rest. I can't say what, but it feels as if there's something in the air. We should be prepared for anything," he warned.

His friend nodded then vanished like the shadow he could be at times.

Blue stood for a long time, waiting for something to happen. Something to answer the question he had in his heart.

It was the next morning when the first thing Blue hadn't expected happened. He had only taken a half dozen steps toward the main lodge when Lance offered a shout. Blue waited for his friend to join him.

"Thanks. I'm still not sure how welcome I am at the house," Lance explained. "I noticed a little more activity than yesterday morning. Figured you better introduce me before I scare anybody."

"What? You think you're the big bad wolf or something?"

Lance grinned. "Or something."

Outside the kitchen doors, a lot of activity was going on. It seemed Sophie had gotten back from her holiday, and she and her little girl were chatting excitedly with Stacy and the other kitchen staff. Perfect. "If you want to be sure you're welcome and well fed, these are the people to introduce you to."

He gestured Lance forward.

They hadn't taken more than a dozen steps when Lance froze on the spot. He tilted his head to one side and took a deep breath.

His eyes widened.

Blue stilled, a wash of something *right* racing over him. Amusement arrived, and anticipation.

Lance was in for the surprise of his life.

Dixie, the most adorable five-year-old dominant Blue had ever met, broke free from her mom's grasp and raced across the lawn, coming to a stop inches away.

She stared up at Lance, head tilted to one side as if slightly confused. "Who *are* you?" she asked.

Lance opened and closed his mouth a few times, but nothing came out.

Dixie's face bloomed into a beautiful little girl smile. "I know who you are." She twisted on the spot and shouted, "*Mamaaaaaa*. Come see. Pretty please?"

Sophie glanced up, smiling at the sweet request. Her gaze drifted to the side and hit on Lance, and she jerked upright. Everything about her looked as if she'd touched a live electric socket. She stepped forward. One foot, then the other and then a half dozen more until she was at top cruising speed, rushing toward them.

She jerked to a stop five feet away, motionless like a statue.

Lance scooped up Dixie when she tugged on his legs, nestling her against his body without looking at her, his gaze locked on Sophie's.

"You'd better get moving," Blue suggested. He put a hand between Lance's shoulders and pushed him forward. "Doesn't look as if you're getting your Amazon, but I guarantee she'll still be perfect for you."

Inarticulate gurgling rose from deep inside Lance as Dixie laid her head on his shoulder and patted his chest softly while singing a little girl tune about hearts and rainbows and wolves with shiny fur.

Lance came to a stop just inches away from Sophie. "Ummm."

Sophie blinked hard. "How?" She shook her head vigorously. "Forget I asked that. Hi."

Blue expected something appropriate like *oh, hello,* in return, or an exchange of names, but what happened was a whole lot more enjoyable to watch. Lance slid his fingers behind Sophie's neck, angled her head, then leaned in and kissed her.

Passionately, thoroughly. As if there was nothing else he was meant to do on this earth but kiss her.

Dixie giggled, patting them both then squirming to be set free. She ran over to Blue, and her smile lit the area. "My mommy has a mate."

"Sure looks that way," he agreed. He lifted her in his arms and tapped her on the nose. "He's a good man. He's gonna make you a great daddy."

Dixie grinned. "I'm going to have a baby brother. *Two* baby brothers."

Well, then, that was a clear declaration from the mouth of babes. Blue eyed her carefully, but she had wiggled to be put down and moved on to skipping in circles around her mother and Lance, singing happily again.

The kissing and the singing attracted attention, but Sophie didn't seem to mind. By the time the two of them came up for air, the rest of the wolves at the lodge had joined them on the lawn.

Jace looked far too cocky and satisfied. "Welcome to the pack. I guess it's official now," he said to Lance.

Sophie's fingers were tangled with Lance's. He still looked a little starstruck, but he tilted his head toward Sophie and smiled down at her. "Looks as if I'm here for good."

Blue had heard of it happening, but it was the first time he'd seen it. Mates were, after all, something that was wildly desired. Insta-mating clearly said the two wolves and their two human sides were not only meant to be together but agreed without a single hesitation.

Which made him very happy for Lance, but once again left waiting.

He examined Stephanie's face. She was watching Sophie and Lance with something that looked like hope and hunger. It came to mind that maybe, just maybe, this would help her take the next step with *him*.

God, Blue hoped so.

~

THE SPONTANEOUS CELEBRATION that occurred after Sophie and Lance's mating was like nothing Stephanie had experienced before.

She knew that wolves were different. Had heard the stories from her sister and friend how the connection between them and their partners was something mostly indescribable.

She'd never registered exactly how *un*-human they were talking about. The sight of Lance and Sophie in total agreement after mere seconds was inspiring and beautiful, and it chilled Stephanie to the core.

A grinning Lance and a very smug Sophie stood before the crowd. Dixie was tucked onto Sophie's hip but held onto her new daddy's shoulder. While there had been no biting—which Stephanie knew was part of the official mating gig—they were clearly a complete unit.

"There's some leftovers from yesterday, but I think we need to pull out steaks and have a breakfast party." Stacy pointed in different directions, snapping out orders, and wolves took off at a run.

"You are getting an extended holiday," Cassidy told Sophie. "And you as well." She included Lance in her smile.

Lance glanced at his mate with affection. "Yes, ma'am, but no ma'am. I have my assignment from your mate, so we won't be taking off anytime soon."

She considered for a moment. "But you will be heading out for a proper honeymoon eventually, understand?

Sophie's cheeks flushed, but her eyes shone with happiness. "We'll be okay." She turned to Lance. "I can't wait to run with you."

Heat flared in his eyes, his wolf near the surface and ready to play. It was also clear that the first chance they had, they were going to get naked for other reasons, as well.

Stephanie wasn't sure how to process the bluntness of that either.

The group moved toward the lodge, and the gathering turned into a breakfast celebration.

When Stephanie finally ended up beside Sophie without anyone close enough to eavesdrop—

Well, okay they were wolves. Everyone *other* than Cassidy and Stacy was still close enough to eavesdrop. Still, politeness dictated that there would be at least the illusion of privacy in their conversation.

Also, Sophie seemed to have read her mind, because the other woman twisted to face Stephanie as she sighed happily. "This must seem odd to you, and you and your family have been very protective of me over the past months. Just to reassure you, I'm happy. I never dreamed this would happen. I am so glad it's him."

"But you don't *know* him," Stephanie said slowly.

Sophie snorted. The indelicate sound seemed wrong for her fine features, and she covered her nose briefly with an embarrassed smile. "I'm sorry, but that sounds so wrong. He's my mate."

"And you talked for less than five minutes."

Sophie shrugged. "It doesn't take time if it's right. I don't need to know what his favourite colour is because I know, as my mate, he wants to make the world a wonderful place for me and for Dixie. He wants to help me do things that will make me a better person. That's what mates do."

"Without more than a kiss—although it *was* smoking hot," Stephanie assured her.

Sophie glanced over and found Lance looking in her direction. Her cheeks flushed in a delightfully modest way even as she winked at him.

She turned back to Steph. "It's a wolf thing, I guess. No,

we haven't done much on the physical side, but honestly that's only part of a relationship. Sex and the rest of it. What's most important is up here." Sophie tapped her temple. "The moment I saw him, I knew he was mine. It'll take time to discover his hopes and dreams. To hear about his life before me. But it doesn't matter how many stories from the past he has, it's what we want for the future that matters the most."

The whole situation made sense if Stephanie thought of it like learning about a foreign country and its unknown customs.

But the last bit Sophie shared—that hit the nail on her fears. "But what if he's unhappy about something in your past? Like, with Dixie's daddy. Won't that be tough on Lance? Or you?"

Understanding lit the young woman's eyes. Sophie caught Stephanie by the arms, holding onto her shoulders and looking wise beyond her years as she answered intently. "Who Dixie's daddy was and what caused me to be a single mom is a part of my story. Lance already loves all of me, unconditionally. He'll be saddened by the things in my past that hurt me, but everything else... How can he do anything except love my past, because it made me who I am today?"

It seemed too good to be true.

It had to have something to do with the magic of mates in the first place, because there was no way this young woman could have that much confidence otherwise, having shared less than a half dozen words with the man before agreeing to be mates.

Thank goodness Stacy called Stephanie away to chop vegetables for salsa, because concentrating with a sharp knife in hand for a while was far better than stewing in her own thoughts.

The celebration involved the staff of Timberwolf Lodge and the leadership of the Jasper pack sprawling easily in lawn chairs and on benches, chatting excitedly. Lance and Sophie were rarely more than a foot apart, exchanging loving glances until Stephanie wanted to roll her eyes.

"You really need to work on your game face," Blue whispered as he slipped onto the bench next to her. "I know insta-mating like this is a wolf thing, but it's real. Stop being a human for a minute and just enjoy the celebration."

She glared at him. "I can't stop being human in case you haven't noticed."

He soothed her patiently. "You know what I mean."

No. No, she did not know what he meant. Or maybe she did, and maybe having a really big fight would be one way to keep him away from her while she struggled with all the other emotions brought up by Lance and Sophie's instant connection.

She opened her mouth to say something smart ass when he slid his fingers into hers. "Can I take you out on a date tonight?"

Time alone with Blue? Bad idea. Plus, they were about to have a fight.

"I'd like that." Stephanie rested her forehead against his. "Well, frack."

He laughed. "Don't worry. I get it."

He kissed her temple, then curled himself around her and held her by his side. Exchanging conversation easily with the others around them. Offering the occasional tidbit, but mostly just being there.

Being Blue. Steadfast. True.

Stephanie couldn't stop looking at Lance and Sophie, though. Because as much as it scared her, there was something huge and wonderful to the experience.

Maybe...

Could she?

A sudden rush of desire hit her. Not sexual, but for connection and unity. She wanted what her sister had. What Cassidy had. What Sophie had accepted in the mere blink of an eye.

So why was she being a fool and not leaping in wholeheartedly to mating Blue?

Because you have secrets that need to stay secret. The words bounced from the back of her brain along with an image of bloody fingers and a violent storm.

"You okay?" Blue rubbed her arm briefly. "You shivered."

"A little cold," she lied, grateful when he curled tighter to her and held her close.

Yeah, there were good reasons to not want another person in her head. But...

Screw it. She was done holding back. Well, not completely, but she and Blue were friends, right? This date tonight was going to be the perfect time to share some truths.

If she dared.

Another sudden thought bounced into her head. This one deep and low and a whole lot less scary. Almost as if someone else had voiced it.

He loves you already. I love you. You are ours, and nothing will change that.

Stephanie sat quietly and wondered.

13

Blue supposed he deserved this in back payment for the grief he'd given his friends when they were wooing their mates. But some things were a step too far.

"If you put one more boring article of clothing on this bed, I'll attach you to the ceiling fan with zip ties," he threatened.

"You'd have to catch me first, and you're too tangled up in Stephanie to be coordinated." Jace threw a Hawaiian shirt aside and glared at the clothes on the bed as if personally offended. "Do you have anything that matches? Do you have anything that's not bright enough to make my eyes bleed?"

"I'm not changing my dressing style to impress Steph." Blue hesitated. "Shit. Do you think I need to change my dressing style to impress Steph?"

Del snorted, reaching into the pile to rescue Blue's favourite red shirt. "If she's your mate, which she is, your bright clothes are already one of her favourite things about you. Wear this one and stop worrying."

"But please, comb your hair. That's an order from Cassidy," Jace offered, sprawling on the bed. He folded his arms behind his head and grinned. "Since you've got the long hippy locks and all, make the most of them."

Blue pulled on his clothes and sighed heavily as he reached for the brush. "This sucks."

Del patted him on the shoulder then dropped to the mattress beside Jace. "It does, but just because Lance and Sophie got together instantly, that doesn't mean you're doing your mating wrong."

Blue frowned as he worked at a knot. "That's not what I was complaining about. I mean it's Tuesday night. Pete's is closed. I have to take Steph to the uber-fancy place at Jasper Park Lodge instead, and we all know it's not nearly as tasty as what Pete offers."

The other two rolled their eyes like teenagers from the past week.

"The sad thing is, he's not lying," Jace pointed out.

"Of course I'm not." Blue checked himself in the mirror. With his hair down around his shoulders, he looked nothing at all like he had during his past military days. Which was probably part of the reason he'd grown it out in the first place.

Huh. Truth telling on himself now. Interesting.

"Have you had any other insights about what's going on?" Del asked. "Or is your Omega super sense still broken?"

"Out of whack, for sure. I don't think I'm permanently busted—it was nice to have the quick flashes of precog with Lance, but it's nothing like usual." Blue pointed at Jace. "And no, I've not gained other superpowers. Other than that one time when I blasted Emma's ass off the mountaintop, I can't call lightning down."

"Too bad. And good. That was a bit too far out there for my liking." Jace eyed him. "I hear François is back in town."

The deep growl that ripped from Blue's throat made Del jump in surprise. "My dear, Blue. How very non-pacifist of you."

"Still don't know how you insist Blue isn't a fighter," Jace said. "You've met Lance. He and Blue were teammates."

Del shrugged. "It's tough to fight against the past seven years of gaudy clothing and grinning exploits."

"That's all behind me now," Blue said. "I'm going to be a grown up member of wolf society and never grin again."

"God, I hope not." Jace shot to his feet and approached Blue. He adjusted his collar slightly then pulled his hair over his shoulder to the back. "You clean up okay. And I don't want another stiff in the pack. Stay yourself, cuz. I like who you are. The only thing that will make you better is when you have Steph by your side."

"And on that note..." Del pulled a rectangular box from his back pocket. "Stacy said you should give Stephanie this."

Blue took the box but shook his head. "I can woo my own mate."

"Take all the help you can get," Jace suggested. Then he too pulled out a present. "Cassidy gave me this for you to give to Steph."

"I'm not handing her gifts when I don't know what's inside," Blue warned. He checked the time then shook his head. "Fine. Let's see what they think is so all-fired important."

Luckily, the boxes were both tied closed with string. Blue slipped the first one free and popped off the lid.

Del snorted. "Cassidy gave you condoms."

With a firm shake of his head, Jace disagreed. "No, Cassidy gave *Steph* condoms. Since Cass knows none are needed to stop disease or pregnancy, it's a message to Steph, not you."

Blue eyed the other box warily. "It's bigger than I like."

Del snorted. "Please. This is amusing enough as it is without you dropping straight-man lines."

Which meant they were all laughing slightly as Blue opened the longer box to reveal a plastic penis. "For fuck's sake."

The cackle that escaped Jace echoed off the wall. "Life-like."

"If your cock is bright pink and green," Del drawled. He eyed Blue. "Considering who we're talking to, it just might be."

"Fuck off." But Blue said it without heat. He picked up the monstrosity and found a remote control under it. "Great. It's rechargeable *and* works at a distance."

"One step ahead of us. I mean, I'm rechargeable, but I like my sex up close and personal." Jace grinned in Blue's face. "Oh, look. Time for you to head out. Have fun and treat your mate-in-training well."

He was going to kill them both. "Thanks."

He quickly closed the gifts and shoved them in his pocket. After one more adjustment, he strolled out the door of the cabin and sauntered to the front door of the lodge.

He had barely raised his knuckles to rap on the door when it swung open and Marvin the moose appeared. Which meant there was not a single inch of living room or foyer visible behind the behemoth.

"Yes?" Marvin asked politely.

Blue raised a brow. "Really?"

Marvin smiled. "I'm teaching Dixie door etiquette." He

shifted his body to one side the barest amount to reveal the little wolf. "Can I help you?"

"Hi, Blue. I'm getting babysat tonight," Dixie announced. "Stephanie looks pretty. Are you taking her somewhere special? My new daddy took my mommy out tonight."

To complete their mating. Lucky devils. Blue squatted and tweaked Dixie's nose. "I'm very happy for your mommy and new daddy. And I am taking Stephanie somewhere special. Can you take me to her, please?"

Dixie thrust out a hand then pushed her little fist into Marvin's massive thigh. "Move, Mr. Marvin. Stephanie needs Mr. Blue."

"Indeed she does," Marvin agreed with a laugh, moving aside. "As much as he needs her."

A shimmer of light shot through the room. Blue stood motionless for a second before realizing it might not have been an Omega reaction. It might have been sunlight flashing off the silver threads in Stephanie's dress.

Holy. Shit. Blue pressed his hand over his heart. "Gorgeous woman."

She stepped forward, the geodesic lines of her dress a kaleidoscope of yellows, oranges, and reds. The supporting lines were black, as if she were wearing a stained glass window. And each bright frame glittered as she moved, the fine lines of contrasting threads catching the light.

She stopped in front of him and eyed him closely. "You are a very pretty man, Blue."

"Is that a good thing? Tell me it's a good thing."

She trailed her fingers through his hair, letting the long strands float over her. "Oh, it's a very good thing. Damn, your hair is softer than mine. What do you use for conditioner?"

"You can compare notes at the restaurant." Cassidy stood a few steps back in the foyer, wide grin firmly in place.

"Come over here, Blue," Stacy ordered from where she waited next to Cassidy.

Blue obeyed, coming to stand next to Steph.

"Smile." Stacy lifted her phone and clicked a picture.

"It's not prom night, mom," Steph complained, curling her arm around Blue's elbow.

Stacy was examining the picture. "You two are so adorable together. Also, I'm making a scrapbook. *Mates-in-training Memories.*"

"Let's go before they start offering unsolicited advice," Steph suggested quietly, tugging him toward the door.

Speaking of which. "One second." He slipped to where Cassidy and Stacy stood. He pulled out the boxes he'd been given and handed them back firmly. "Thanks. But I have this under control."

Stacy raised a brow.

"Don't," Blue warned. "No comments, not one. Go find your guys and torment them."

"But you're so much easier to get a rise out of right now," Cassidy pointed out.

"Say goodnight, ladies," Blue ordered, catching Steph by the hand and making a break for it.

"Good night, ladies." Stacy snickered. "Have fun. Don't do anything that—"

"Run for it," Steph ordered.

They made their escape as laughter drifted behind them.

❧

Blue led her toward a shiny Blue Mustang that made her blink. She'd never seen it before.

"New wheels?" she asked, because focusing on the car was safer than thinking about how good it felt to hold his hand.

"Secret wheels," he told her, opening the door and waiting for her to climb in. "I don't let Jace or Del drive Birdie. The easiest way to do that is to keep her at my house."

"Birdie?"

He grinned. "Bluebird of happiness."

Stephanie mindlessly did the things usually done when entering a car, but the comment flashed in her brain like a big neon sign on high alert.

The instant Blue sat, she pounced on it. "*Your* house. I'm terrible. I cannot believe that I've been in Jasper since June and have never once asked about where you lived before."

Blue waited until they were heading up the long hill toward town before speaking. "I'm mostly to blame for that," he said. "I'm the one who took over one of the cabins so I could stay on the property."

"So that you were closer to do all the work you've done to help us."

His fingers wrapped around hers. "No. That was a side benefit. I moved so I'd be closer to you."

The quiver in her belly was followed hard by warmth flowing over her like a big hug. "Because you knew we were mates."

He squeezed her fingers lightly.

They sat in silence for a few minutes as Stephanie let that sink in a little harder. He'd moved his entire life to be near her, all the while never pressuring her to change herself.

You are ours.

She glanced at Blue, but he hadn't said anything.

Great. Now she was hearing voices. More distraction needed. "Where are we going?"

"Sadly, not to Pete's." He grinned. "Although we have an invite from him for next week. He's doing some menu changes and wants us as guinea pigs."

"Yes, please." She made some guesses. "So tonight is pizza? Pasta?"

"Steak." Blue nodded at her hum of approval. "I'm not trying to go all fancy to impress you..." He met her gaze. "Not unless it's working."

Stephanie laughed with him before realizing he was only sort of kidding. "You don't need to impress me," she told him softly. "We're more than friends, remember?"

They held hands the rest of the trip. Blue rubbed his thumb over the back of her knuckles in a teasing caress that sent shivers of anticipation up her spine.

While Blue might not have intended to impress her, the location was fantastic. Like Timberwolf Lodge but intended for humans. With soaring wooden beams and enormous log timbers, it could be a sister to the place Stephanie now called home.

Home. The challenge.

"How do you think things went with Mrs. Wilson? You escorted her granddaughter home, didn't you?" They had just been seated, Blue at her right hand. The tiny half-circle table had an epic view over Elizabeth Lake, with small decorative lights tangled in all the nearby trees. "Wow. We need to do some rearranging at Timberwolf Lodge. Maybe some extra outside seating that faces the lake for the spring."

"Good idea. We'll mention it to Cass tomorrow." Blue

glanced at the wine list then placed it on the table. "In terms of the Wilsons...I'm not sure."

The concern was a marked contrast to his usually happy expression. "What's wrong?"

He shook his head. "I'll tell you, but let's order first. You want to pick the wine?"

"Why don't you do it?" Some evil impulse hit, and Stephanie lifted her chin. "In fact, you should order the entire meal. I'm going to relax and enjoy the view."

His lips twitched. "Sure. I think I saw prairie oysters as an appetizer."

She snickered. "If you eat it, I'll eat it."

Blue pulled a small notebook from his pocket. "Challenge accepted."

He quickly wrote their order without letting her read it, then ripped the page from the book and handed it to the waiter when he returned.

Then Blue took her hand in his and stared into her eyes. "As an Omega, I usually have certain skills. Like being able to really get to the root of emotions in the pack. We don't have tons of trouble with depression or anxiety as wolves, but it does happen. I can feel the emotions of another wolf to the degree that I know what they need for help. Space, or a hug, or a good old butt-kicking."

"Handy skill." She frowned. "Usually?"

He nodded. "It's fuzzy these days. And when it comes to you, while I can still sense your emotions, the play-by-play book isn't spitting out specific directions. I'm trying to be who you need me to be, but I don't have a Magic 8 Ball. No more than the average wolf."

His trying wasn't the problem. "Us not being mates yet is not because of anything you've done," she assured him.

A gentle shrug lifted his shoulders. "You asked about

the Wilsons. What I read from Ermeline was some curiosity and a whole lot of lingering anger. She doesn't really have a reason to be mad at us—except for her niece."

Stephanie couldn't remember all the wolf connections, and then it hit. "Emma. We banished her."

"For good reasons. No wolf pack would argue the decision. But people sometimes feel deeply when family is involved." Blue sat back and gestured to the side. "Our wine is here."

The Syrah was delicious, but Stephanie was distracted by Blue's news. "I suppose, in one way, it's good to have the heads up that Ermeline isn't all peaches and cream about us right now. That gives us time to adjust her opinion."

"It does. It's good you suggested the reach out."

Blue changed the topic, telling her about past holiday seasons at the lodge, with skating on the lake and toboggan runs down the big hill in both human and wolf forms. They ate calamari and a goat cheese and fig salad. The steaks that arrived for their main course had Steph's mouthwatering.

"Bacon wrapped filet for me?"

Blue nodded. "And you get to steal slices of my tenderloin with peppercorn gravy and saskatoon reduction."

Yum. "I'm going to end up in a food coma."

He winked. "Don't. You still owe me a foot rub."

"Since when?" Although she was already slicing into her steak, the meat all but melting on her tongue. "Never mind. I'm in heaven. Foot rubs are always available in heaven."

Blue cut off a piece of his steak for her, dipping half in one sauce, half in the other. "Hey. For you."

He held his fork up and she leaned in and took it,

wrapping her lips around the tongs. His eyes dilated as he stared at her mouth.

Between the food and the expression on his face, she was about to go into raptures. She swallowed hard. "Behave," she whispered.

"I *am* behaving. Noting how I'm not currently picking you up and ravishing you against the wall?"

She really hated that the plan sounded like a very good idea. Change of topic.

"Tell me more about your auntie and uncle," she suggested. "The ones who lived at Timberwolf Lodge before us."

He raised a brow but gave in, telling her stories while they enjoyed their steaks then demolished an enormous piece of flourless chocolate cake.

Stephanie was staring into the final swallows of her wine when her curiosity could no longer be contained, and the words simply burst free.

"Blue? Do you think there's some connection between us? Like...something Omega-ish?" Thinking of his ability to sense emotions, maybe if she could sense them, she could hide them as well.

Blue hesitated. "Because you want there to be or you don't want there to be?"

She sighed. "You're far too insightful at times."

"Nothing to do with being Omega." He touched his fingers to the edge of her cheek. "Everything to do with knowing I care about you. I don't need magical Omega senses to tell when you're worried. Please, sweetheart. Trust me."

Which she did. Completely. "It's me I don't trust," she whispered.

Secrets. Secrets needed to be kept.

Steph, secrets need to be shared that other voice told her firmly.

She shook her head. "Why do I keep hearing—?" Then all questions vanished because outside the window, a ghost walked by. A shot of dizziness struck, followed by panic. "Oh my God."

Blue grabbed her hand, trying to follow her gaze. "What's wrong?"

Stephanie pointed at the man walking along the path by the lake. "That's— Well, he looks exactly like Stacy's ex-husband, Porter."

Which she knew was impossible. Knew to the core of her being because she'd seen his dead body at her feet.

The wolf by her side snapped to attention. "It might be Porter, but it's more likely Dwight, the man who claimed to be his brother. Where?"

She nodded. "Walking that direction."

Blue considered for a split second, then tugged her to her feet. "I need to follow him. You want to stay here or—"

"I'm coming with you." She motioned for the waiter as they moved quickly to the exit. "I'll stay out of your way, but I need to do this."

Blue dropped a roll of cash on the counter, then they slipped outside into the cool fall night.

14

Stalking his prey with Stephanie by his side wasn't ideal. Not until Blue realized that stalking wasn't the correct plan of attack under these circumstances.

He tucked her hand onto his elbow and slowed them to a stroll. Just another couple out for a walk by the lake on this gorgeous cool night.

"You still see him?" Blue asked, leaning closer to her.

"On the path to the right. He's looking around as if he's a tourist. Which I guess he is, all things considered." Steph tightened her grip on his arm. "Why is he here?"

"That's one thing we'll find out," Blue promised. "But first, we confirm he's staying in the accommodations that Lance tracked down. Keeping an eye on him will be easier if we start with that."

When Dwight paused to sit on a bench by the lake, Blue tugged Steph against him, her back to the nearest tree.

She looked up at him with shining eyes. Some of it fear, but higher still was the desire he scented, the pulse of her heart at her throat a wild rhythm.

The desire was too much to ignore. Even with the

fucked-up situation, he had to do it. "You look as if you need something," he told her.

"What?" She tried to peer as far to the side as possible with her peripheral vision, but he pressed a hand to her cheek and turned her to face him.

"This."

He eased in. Slow enough their breath mingled at first, the lingering taste of sweet chocolate combining with the distinct flavour of his mate.

Steph gripped his shirt collar with both hands, the words gusting over his cheek. "Should we do this?"

"It's not a question of should, it's a question of necessity. I need you, Steph. Like I need air." Blue kissed her then, the eager response of her lips against his making all his repressed desires shoot sky high.

Steph slid her tongue against his, retreated. He responded by pressing her tighter to the tree with his body, the soft curve of her breasts accepting him like a heated pillow. His hardening cock hit the slope of her belly, and the entire time, he nibbled on her bottom lip. Stole tastes from her mouth. Tangled their tongues and fought to keep from hiking her leg over his hip and grinding on her like a rutting animal.

She fisted her hands in his hair and tugged him back a fraction of an inch. "You still see Dwight?"

"Yes." Thank God, the man was admiring the scenery. "Kiss me again," Blue ordered.

Stephanie obliged. God, he was so hot he was one step away from blowing up, and they were only kissing. How was he going to keep his shit together when they actually got into bed?

That was a problem for another time, though, with his mate all sexy and tousled under his body weight. Her sexual need scented the air like the best of aphrodisiacs, and Blue wallowed in it.

Movement his wolf cautioned.

Blue pulled back from Steph, their gazes meeting. "We are not done with this," he warned.

She nodded rapidly, even as she twisted to check out their quarry. "He's walking," she whispered.

"So we'll walk, too. Not too close, just in case."

For him, it was natural to slip back into stealth mode. And as if she'd been doing this all her life, Steph tucked her fingers into his elbow and strolled at his side. Not so fast they'd close the distance between them and their target. Not so slow that if Dwight turned a corner they'd have to rush and potentially give away their position.

The man clearly had no tracking abilities himself and very little sense of self-preservation. He walked up to one of the rental cottages by the lake and let himself in. A moment later, the light in the living space came on.

Blue tucked Stephanie closer to his side, away from the cabin. "Keep going. I want to be sure he can't get out unless he crawls out a window."

"They don't have back doors," she whispered. "I looked into it when I was doing comparisons for Timberwolf Lodge.

Good to know. He squeezed her shoulders, then guided her far enough away he could still see the door but Dwight couldn't see them. "I'm going to call in backup. They'll continue surveillance for the rest of the night."

"We could stay," Steph offered, even as a shivered rippled over her.

"We're on a date, he said firmly. He quickly texted the number of a pack member Del given him. When he got an affirmation that the guard was on the way, he eased Steph to the side, tugging her against him once again. "They'll be here soon. I have some really good ideas of how to pass the time."

She raised a brow, glancing back at the cabin with concern. "But what if—"

Kissing the worry off her lips was the best of all solutions.

He kept one ear open, but there was no way Dwight could leave without him noticing. Even if taking charge of Stephanie's mouth was hugely distracting, Blue was capable of multitasking. Especially since not multitasking would have meant not kissing her.

The arrival of his pack mate only a few minutes later was a grateful event, though. Blue pulled away from Steph's mouth, humming happily as he stroked a finger over her lower lip. "Delicious."

"It's the cake," she teased.

"It's you," he insisted. "Come on. The guard arrived. She's in her wolf and will be able to keep a close eye on our unwelcome guest."

Steph dipped her chin. She bit her lip then straightened slightly as if deciding. "Take me to your place?"

"My cabin at Timberwolf?"

"Your place here in Jasper. By your workshop."

He hadn't seen that one coming. "Okay. There's no food there and not much to drink."

Steph patted his chest lightly. "I'm not hungry. Not that way."

Urgent need rushed in. Picking her up and sprinting the entire way to his place wasn't the cool-and-collected image he liked to portray.

But then again—this was Steph. She knew him. She would know all of him, inside and out, eventually. Forget cool and collected. She smelled like anticipation and pleasure, and he couldn't wait to meet her needs.

He did wait until they were in the trees and out of sight of any wandering public before scooping her off her feet and making a break for it.

Steph laughed as she wrapped her arms around his neck and clung like a vine. "Blue. What are you doing? Your car—"

"My place is close enough to here we'll be there in a few minutes. My car needs a little time out in the world. She'll be fine in the parking lot. It'll be an adventure."

She was laughing harder now, the sound bright and warm on the cool night air. Her hold on him was tight, but not as if she were afraid...as if she didn't want to let him go.

Moments later he approached his house from the lakeside, lowering her gently to her feet and taking her by the hand to guide her to the back deck. "Welcome. The house is small, and the workshop's a mess, but it's all mine."

It's all hers now, his wolf said clearly.

Yes, but one thing at a time, Blue warned his other side. *Not too fast, still.*

You are going too slow, his inner beast growled.

Blue ignored...himself?...and walked up the short set of stairs by her side. "Doors are all unlocked."

"You're trusting."

"I'm an Omega. No wolf is going to come in unwelcome, and I spray *Humans Be Gone* on a regular basis to stop the rest of them."

Stephanie offered a startled glance then rolled her eyes at his wink. "Tease."

"I can't explain it, but I never lock doors. Either people stay out, or they were meant to come in. It's all good." And his mysterious open door policy wasn't what he wanted to spend time discussing right now.

She pivoted, taking in the suntanning loungers he'd placed in the middle of the deck that stretched the entire length of the house. The right side held his barbeque and the cozy picnic table only big enough for four.

She hesitated then led him to far left where two comfy chairs were nestled by his gas firepit. Behind them were the sliding glass doors to his bedroom.

Steph slid the door open and pushed aside the curtains. The deep red quilt on his bed was neatly in place, and comfortable pillows were stacked at the head of the king-size bed. She took a deep breath then faced him. "The quilt isn't bright yellow?"

"I'll buy one if you'd like."

A wash of need rushed from her, but she shook her head. Stepping into the room then twisting, Steph met his gaze. "You said you needed me. I need you, too."

Thank God. Blue stepped into the room and joined his mate.

THIS WAS ALL WRONG. Stephanie had meant to start by telling him why she was so scared.

Oh, she wasn't going to tell him everything, but she figured at least the truth about *being* scared would explain why they had to stop one step before their completing mating. Becoming mates?

However it was said, they were not going to do it.

Except they were totally going to *do it*.

Every inch of her craved his touch, and with the way he

was looking at her right now, she was one Bic flick away from igniting.

There was hunger in his eyes, but also that quintessential thing that made him *Blue*. Amusement tangled up with stubborn strength. "I'm going to take care of you," he promised, "but if I do anything you don't like, just tell me to stop."

"I feel as if I might spend a lot more time telling you to *go*," she teased. "Why are you standing all the way over there?"

Blue had barely entered the room. He slid the door closed, leaving the curtains open so the lights outside shone in, casting golden fingers over the bed. "I've been dreaming about this for months, Steph. I'm not going to rush."

Then, as if in complete opposition to his intentions, he crowded her. Instinct made her rush to retreat. The back of her legs hit the bed and she sat, looking up at him as his eyes glowed with fire.

But it wasn't scary; it was totally fun. And Stephanie dropped her shoes and wiggled onto the bed, trying to get away and knowing she couldn't.

Blue was over her in a second, strong arms braced on either side of her head. His body rested over hers, hips cradled between her legs. Perfectly intimate, the long hard length of his cock pressed to her clit. Layers of fabric might have separated them, but they were still right *there*. Fully on board and enjoying every second.

"I'd like to be naked," Stephanie suggested.

"Great by me," Blue told her, his hair falling around them like a curtain. He let his gaze drift down the part of her torso he wasn't actively in contact with. "Strip."

She waited for him to back away, but if anything, he nestled even tighter. A heavy throb had begun between her legs, sexual tension rising. A different kind of delicious. Stephanie met his gaze as she reached down to catch the edge of her skirt with her fingertips.

Inching the fabric up only worked so well. She had to wiggle, squirming and pressing herself closer to him. Tormenting them both in the sweetest way possible.

He leaned on his elbow and used his right hand to slide behind her back and undo the zipper of her dress. That was the only concession he made to helping her undress. That, and undoing her bra so quickly she wondered if he'd used a claw to cut through the fabric.

"What are you going to do once I'm naked and you still have all your clothes on?" she teased.

"I'm going to finish having my dessert."

Another heavy pulse between her legs.

By the time he helped slip the fabric over her head, they were both panting, and not from exertion. Her skin felt as if she were being tickled by a thousand fireflies, and the look in his eyes—

Blue cupped her face with his right hand and kissed her. Long and lingering, while his fingers took a slow journey down her neck and over her collarbone before sliding into place over her breast.

His mouth followed that same path, landing on her nipple with a soft wet lick and a gentle nip that shot her arching toward him.

A low growl escaped him. He moved a little quicker, hands cupping both breasts as he teased and kissed and licked until both her nipples were so tight and sensitive she didn't know if she should push him away or drag him closer.

Blue rested his head against her belly and breathed deeply. "Damn it, Steph. Your scent is so fucking good. I can smell your need for me, and after all this time, I'm about to lose control."

She combed her fingers through his hair and met his frustrated expression with a smile. "Go ahead and lose control. From what I hear, you wolves are kind of like the Energizer Bunny. You'll be ready to go again in a few minutes."

That's when Stephanie learned it was dangerous to suggest her wolf should *go ahead and lose control*.

He didn't hurt her, but he lost any edge of civility. Scraping his teeth over her belly, he thrust his hands under her hips and raised her to his mouth. This was no gentle licks and teasing tongue play. This was a full-on feasting, because he was a starving wolf and she was the feast he'd earned. Stephanie tightened her fingers in his hair and held on for the ride. It was her only choice, because unless she wanted to physically wrestle control back—*ha!*—the only thing she had the strength to do was enjoy.

He took her up hard, and he took her up fast, dragging an orgasm from her body in under a minute. When she would have pulled him over her to do the next thing, he went and did it all over again. Sharp little nips that sent electric storms over her skin. Intense sucking motions that were going to leave her a whole lot of love bites.

Good thing it wasn't summer and she didn't plan on wandering around in a bikini any time soon.

The third orgasm left her shaking, clutching the sheets for dear life. "*Blue*. No more. I need you."

He rose slightly, wiping his fingers over his mouth as he stared down her naked body as if considering what to nibble on next. "I'm not done."

Damn it. She couldn't take much more of this. She contorted herself up as far as possible to grip the front of his shirt. Jerking her hands apart, the top buttons and some fabric gave way with a satisfying sound. "Then don't be *done*, but first, get your cock inside me."

World's fastest strip show.

Stephanie had barely registered him rising from her, when he was back, every inch of his muscular frame pressed to hers, and his cock right there—

Blue rocked his hips, coating himself in the moisture her multiple orgasms had produced. "Steph?" He stared into her eyes.

She touched his face briefly, giving him another order along with her clear consent. "Look down. Watch as you push inside me. Look at *us* becoming one."

Heat flared again, and mischief, as he caught her hand and guided it between their bodies. Their fingers both right there, sliding over his cock and the edge of her pussy as he slowly but firmly connected them. His cock slid all the way in until they were skin to skin from that point down, his torso still hovering over hers so she could see everything.

Intimate, incredible.

She was so, so full, and so exactly where she needed to be. "That's good," she whispered.

"It's fucking fantastic," he corrected, amusement curling the edges of his lips. He lifted his hips and lowered them, the in and out motion of his cock against her core stroking with such perfect pressure, pleasure rose all over again.

He picked up the pace, and that's when Stephanie gave up all pretense of being ready for this. She'd expected a fast roll in the hay. This was need and urgency and power barely restrained. His hips pulsed in a frantic tempo, muscles of his torso gone rigid with pleasure.

She spiraled upward. Floating toward some impossible goal—too many orgasms to count and yet another on the way? She pressed her fingers to his shoulders and savoured the heat of him. Over her and around her and in her.

Blue dropped onto her even as he continued to fuck her, their torsos sliding together while extreme pleasure rippled over her skin, and she was breaking. His mouth caught her cry of delight, his tongue and teeth swallowing the sound of his name from her lips.

He slowed, the tight squeeze of sex round his cock making him shudder until he stiffened and joined her in release.

Breathing heavy, kissing softer now, his cock still heavy inside her, Stephanie sighed as all the happy little endorphins raced to her extremities and turned her into a puddle of goo. "That was very good *not in control* sex."

Blue nuzzled her neck, chuckling softly. "I thought I managed to pull myself under control pretty good. Next time we'll go for out of control."

God help her. "Cuddle me first? Because my hoo-ha is tingling so hard I need time to let the blood flow return to normal through my body, or I might pass out."

"Can't have you passing out," he agreed with a laugh, patting her bottom. "Poor hoo-ha."

He rolled, and she ended up sprawled on top of him. Still connected, but the thick pressure between her legs slowly fading. Stephanie pressed her palms to his chest and examined his face.

Contentment painted his features with happiness.

She kissed him gently then laid her head down and concentrated on deep, even breathing. She had some truths to share, but right now, this moment—

This was too important to interrupt with anything.

15

———

A soft, high-pitched sound woke him. Blue pulled himself to full attention without twitching a muscle. He didn't want to disturb the woman in his arms.

Only Stephanie was the reason for the noise. Barely an hour after she'd fallen asleep in his arms, she shivered, rocking from head to toe as a whimper escaped. When she curled tighter into his chest, Blue swore softly then cradled her closer.

"Steph, sweetheart. Wake up."

He got another whimper, her fingers twitching as if trying to flick something off.

Blue held on tight as he patted her shoulder more firmly. "Steph. Wake up. You're having a bad dream."

A sudden gasp exploded from her lips. She thrust her palms against his chest so hard he'd have had bruises if he wasn't a shifter. In the small space she'd created between them, Steph made to wiggle away. "No. *Never.*"

"It's Blue. I'm here," he insisted, letting her free to escape if that's what she needed.

Too slow, his wolf said in a frantic tone. *My job,* he added reproachfully.

An uncomfortable jolt rushed through Blue. A similar sensation to when he shifted, only he was still standing on two feet—so to speak. Still in human form.

But Steph's eyes flew open, her mouth open slightly as she fought to focus on him. "Blue?"

"Yes, baby. It's me. You're safe. You were having a nightmare."

"Not a nightmare." She cringed, shaking her head. "I heard you."

"Because I'm right here."

Steph pushed up on an elbow, twisting to glance around the room. She let out a huge, relieved breath, then met his gaze. A crease lay between her brows, but at least she wasn't shaking anymore. "No, I heard you. In here." She tapped her temple.

What the hell?

First things first, though. "You okay? You were scared by something."

"Old...nightmare." She swallowed hard, her eyes widening. "Oh." She examined his lips. "You're not talking. But *you're* talking to me."

Blue frowned. "What?"

I'm taking care of our mate, his wolf informed Blue. *If she's not alone, she won't be afraid.*

Oh shit, more weird shifter tricks. "My wolf is talking to you? What did he tell you?" Blue asked.

She nodded. "He said he's there for me until you and I are fully mates."

The expression on her face—he was sure his was also full of confusion and disbelief. "This isn't typical," he warned her. "I mean, I *know* talking to each other mind to mind is possible with mates, but *I* can't hear what he's saying."

You don't need to hear. Stephanie needed me, so I came. I'll deal with this side, you deal with yours.

Thanks for the sentiment, Blue offered, *but going solo like you've done is not really helping.*

She's not scared anymore. His wolf damn near gloated as he said it.

Blue shoved aside his frustration and caught Steph's fingers in his. "Uncertain Omega wolf tricks aside, are you okay?"

"I think so." She adjusted position, putting her back against the headboard of his bed, and tucking the sheets around her like a toga. Which was sad because he'd been enjoying the naked part, although not the afraid part. She paused as if listening to another voice that he couldn't hear. "This isn't typical?"

"Nope. One of a kind, it appears. You and me."

She nodded slowly as if considering. "You and me. We had sex, but we're not fully mates yet. That's what furry Blue said."

He shook his head. "Just excellent sex. Or I thought it was excellent sex."

Despite her confusion, amusement broke through. "Most excellent. But the mate part, it's not complete, yet your wolf is in my head."

"Somehow, yup."

"Okay." She took a deep breath. "Okay."

Not really, but he'd have to fake it for now. "Do you want to get up? Get dressed and go home?" Hopefully not. "Want a backrub, or that foot rub I owe you?"

She lifted herself upright as if preparing for battle. "I

want to talk if that's okay. I need to tell you something. FB says it's important."

"FB?"

"Furry Blue," she offered.

Blue snorted. "He's trouble."

"You're a matched set." Steph worried her bottom lip. "I didn't want to tell you this. It's been haunting me since the moment you blurted out that we were mates."

God, this sounded ominous. "I'm sorry."

She shook her head. "You've done nothing wrong. But the girls told me about their connections with their mates, and..." She'd been curling in on herself as she spoke, but again, she forced herself upright as if fighting to be brave. "I've done things in the past that I've never told anyone. And I'm worried that if people know"—she met his gaze again—"that if *you* know, you'll think less of me. That you'll be horrified or disgusted."

A slim glimmer of hope lit his heart. "Steph? You know I was in the military for a while, yes?"

She nodded. "You told us stories a couple times by the fire."

"I told you the PG versions, and the ones more about the places we traveled than the things I saw. The things I did."

"Military stuff isn't normally very nice." She swallowed. "You're an honorable man. Shifter."

"I try to be," Blue agreed. "But I was a shifter with a job to do in some dangerous places. I didn't let my team down, and that meant there were times and actions I don't like to remember."

"Then don't." She made a face. "Except I know that's easy to say and hard to do. Not thinking about some things is impossible. But Blue, what you did—I'd never judge you for it."

"Thanks." He lowered his voice to a caress. "Then why does it sound as if you're judging *yourself?*"

Nail on head. Steph sucked in so much air she looked ready to burst before deflating on her exhale. "I don't regret what I did, but I wish it had never happened. Does that make sense?"

"Totally." Impulsively, he stood. He grabbed one of his shirts from the cupboard and tossed it at her. "Pull this on. We need hot chocolate with hootch and a nice fire to curl up in front of. And then I'm going to hold you until you know that I am yours, and FB is yours, and you can tell us anything, and nothing will ever change how much we love you."

She pressed a hand to her chest, eyes brimming with moisture. "You love me?"

"Yup." Blue leaned down and gently wiped a tear before stepping back and pulling on a pair of boxers. "Because we're mates, but first and foremost because we're more than friends. Yes, I love you. I adore you, desire you, and crave you. Now get dressed because I also want to hug the stuffing out you, ASAP."

She was laughing as she pulled on his shirt. Then she took his hand and followed him into the living room.

As they worked companionably to make drinks and light the fire, Stephanie considered hard. Blue's words tapped on her guilty conscience with the enthusiasm of a woodpecker digging in old trees for juicy bugs.

He was right.

She didn't judge him for any actions that had kept his teammates or the people around them safe. Why was she still allowing *her* truth to torment her?

Because you should never have had to do it in the first place. The voice in her head was deep and kind.

Knowing it was Blue's wolf—which meant *Blue*—talking in her head made it better and stranger at the same time.

You know what I did? Stephanie asked hesitantly.

Not the details, but I know your heart. And your emotions are tangled. Relief and fear and strength—you are so strong, Stephanie. We're glad to have a strong mate.

Stephanie stirred the chocolate one more time, adding healthy shots of Baileys. Then she sucked in her courage and joined Blue in front of the fire.

He accepted the mug she passed him, placing it to the side then patting the carpet to his left. "Saved you a spot."

"Thanks, but I see a better place." She crawled on top of him.

Rearranging herself in his lap until she was comfortable sent him chuckling. "Make yourself at home." He pressed a kiss to her temple. "And I mean that absolutely."

"I know. I'm *starting* to truly understand." Stephanie rested her head on his shoulder. "You were a soldier. Special shifter forces?"

"There are people in the know in the military. If you want to make the best use of your resources, you put your wolves and cats and other shifters in the same platoon and use *all* their skills." He stroked her hair, and though not meeting his eyes, she still felt his emotion. His deep conviction that what he was sharing was true. "I'm glad that time is done now, but it made me who I am today."

An echo of what Sophie had said earlier. About the past being done but still being important.

She braced herself, then began. "I'm a simple person, Blue. I'm not super smart, or strong, or creative. I didn't go to college or university, but I've always found a way to make ends meet. Giving people spa treatments and massages makes me happy and earns me money. But most importantly, it's let me be there for Stacy and Cassidy. They are my most important job every day. To be there for them is everything."

"I can tell. You love them unconditionally, and it shows."

Stephanie patted his chest then leaned back enough she could look him in the eyes. "When Stacy married the first time, her husband was a great guy. Gone a lot, which meant our gal-group stayed intact and close. When James died and we discovered Colt was a shifter, we got even closer."

Blue stayed silent, running his fingers through her hair. The sensation of being petted soothed her nerves.

"Porter changed that. I hated him from the first minute I laid eyes on him. When he sneakily tried to separate us and isolate Stacy, I knew something was wrong. Stacy eventually realized his nice guy side was a ploy, and she took the steps to get out."

God, was she really going to tell him this? Tell him everything?

You need to say it, Steph. Furry Blue said in her head. *We love you. No matter what.*

I'm scared, she admitted.

It's okay to be scared. It's not okay to be cruel to yourself. Let go, he urged. *We have big arms to catch you.*

Stephanie met Blue's eyes. He had one brow raised in a question. "Sorry. FB is giving me advice."

"Good advice?"

"Yeah. He's telling me to get over myself and spit it out."

I did not. I was far more eloquent than that, Furry Blue protested, which made Stephanie snort.

She clutched Blue's fingers. "Okay, spitting it out. When Stacy gave Porter divorce papers, I knew it wasn't going to go over well. I just *knew*. I think I'd seen signs of his temper more often than either Cass or Stacy because I always seemed to end up coming or going past him when he was losing it. I don't know why. I'd shortcut through the back alley and find him cursing and smashing things into the back fence. I did a job one time for a neighbour then impulsively took a short cut and spotted him chopping down part of Stacy's garden, swinging a machete as if he were in the jungle, his face mottled with rage. He told Stacy they'd had vandals who ruined it. I told her the truth, and I think that's when Stacy realized she needed to get out."

Blue's expression hardened.

"It was a terrible day with a huge storm raging outside. Cass and I were at the house to support and protect Stacy. Cassidy had a friend in the local police force, and she'd agreed to be there, just in case. Picture the three of us, one in official police uniform, all lined up in a row to make sure Porter didn't do anything stupid when Stacy gave him the papers."

"The kids? Just Colt and Blaze back then, right?"

"Yeah. They were at a friend's for a playdate to make sure they were safe. And I'm glad, because if you had seen Porter's face..." The memories were rushing in, clear as ever. "If he could have reached out right then and strangled Stacy, he would have."

"I thought Porter got the divorce papers then left. He hasn't been seen since."

"I went after him," she confessed.

Blue jolted upright. "You what?"

"He pulled on a sad smile—so, so fake—said he understood, and quietly walked out. Cassidy and Jen stayed with Stacy, but I sensed something was wrong, so I slipped out after him. I was soaked in seconds, the rain pouring down and thunder going off so close it rattled the house. I spotted Porter slipping into the garden shed at the back of the property."

Every muscle in Blue's body had gone rigid. "Steph."

She had to finish now. Had to get it all out. "The door was ajar, so I peeked in. He was pulling a gun out of a drawer. I must have made a noise of some kind because he turned and lunged. He caught my wrist and hauled me into the shed with him."

Closing her eyes, she could picture it clearly. Porter's rage and anger. And lust as he'd dropped his gaze over her.

Show me, Furry Blue demanded. *I'm here. You're safe.*

Suddenly, Stephanie was in two places at the same time. She knew Blue's arms were around her. That FB was in her head, his cool deep voice as good as a hug.

But she was also back there—back in a time and place when she'd walked into the garden shed because she *knew* Porter planned to kill her sister.

"You shouldn't have come here," the Porter in her memories said. "You could have died quickly with the rest of them. All except Colt, of course. That kid's going to turn into a wolf one day, and I'm going to find out how. But since you're here, before I get rid of the rest of them, I may as well enjoy myself first."

He jerked her toward him.

Stephanie moved without thinking. He might have a tight grip on her right hand, but that didn't mean much to her. The countertop to her left was covered with small bedding pots and gardening hand tools. She swept her hand over it, palm landing on something hard and cool, and she clutched it tightly. A small rake fell to the floor, and a trowel, black plastic pots flying as she thrust the razor sharp dandelion knife at Porter, forward into his belly and up as hard as she could.

Porter's eyes widened and he roared, pain rearranging his twisted features.

Stephanie kept her fingers tight on the knife she'd grabbed off the counter with her left hand, twisting it toward his lungs before jerking it free. "Never. You can't touch my sister, or my nephews, or my friends. You won't touch any of them ever again."

She stepped back, escaping as he grabbed for her. Overhead, lightning flashed against the glass of the window, thunder instantly echoing in the small space and drowning out Porter's screams of pain.

He fell to the ground, hands over his belly as blood poured through his fingers. Stephanie tipped over the storage shelf to her right, the packages of potting soil smacking Porter lightly an instant before the solid wooden frame crushed him to the ground.

She remembered standing there, waiting silently. Fully expecting he'd roar again and rise like a monster to destroy her before finishing off her family.

The storm assaulted the shed with thunder and lightning for ten minutes before she saw the line of blood trickling out from under the toppled shelf. Her hands were covered in blood, glistening red shining in the silver flashes of lightning through the window.

I'm here. You're not alone. FB's words broke the spell,

and Stephanie slowly became aware of the here and now. The memories faded, the images slipping into haze.

"You saved them." Blue whispered the words against her temple. He held her tighter than before, his breathing uneven. "And you saved yourself. God, Steph. You were so brave."

"I killed him." Blood on her hands. Her fingernails torn up and ragged by the time she finished dealing with his body. "I hauled his body into his truck, manhandled my moped into the back, then cleaned up the mess in the shed including the gun and ammo. I called Stacy to tell her I had a job to do—she thought I meant a massage, I guess. Then I got out of there."

That was the part that really haunted her. How easy it had been to calculate the next moves.

"Where did you hide him?" Blue asked quietly.

"We had a friend with a place in the lake district. It's not a nice place—very remote and isolated. I rigged the truck with Porter's body in it to drive off the edge of a cliff into a section of lake that's undeveloped." She looked Blue straight in the eye. "Killing him? That was impulsive and instinctive. I deliberately did everything else. I hid it. I planned and I figured out how not to get caught. Driving to the cabin took hours, and I never once considered turning myself in. I knew the only way they would be safe was if Porter was dead, and with Colt being a shifter... I couldn't risk bringing the police into it. I even faked Porter's signature on the divorce papers. Told Stacy I'd make sure he signed them."

He looked for a second as if he was going to protest then reconsidered and nodded slowly. "That doesn't make what you did wrong. Not in my books."

Exhaustion flowed over her like a weighed blanket. Even so, the expression on his face—she had to ask him.

"You still love me?" God. Her voice shook as if she was on the verge of tears. And maybe she was. Losing him now would destroy her.

Blue cupped her cheek in his big strong palm. "I love you more now than before. And tomorrow, I'll learn another reason to love you more. It's not going away, Steph. This thing between us will only grow."

Humans use so many words, FB complained. *Our love is forever. Period.*

Which meant Stephanie's heart welled up with happiness at the sweet, sweet gift from Blue, and she tipped over into laughter at the dry bluntness of FB.

She threw her arms around Blue's neck. "I love you, too."

Then she cried. For all the days and months and years she'd had to hold it inside. For the weight she'd carried that she now got to share. She let go of the guilt and instead accepted the love she'd been offered.

One watery sniffle at a time.

16

———

Blue held Stephanie until she squirmed to be let up. Then he kissed her tenderly and sent her to the shower. "Wash away your tears. I'll line up the next episode in our current glom."

"More throwdown? Awesome." Stephanie hesitated. "You're not going to tell Jace, are you? Aren't there rules about not keeping secrets from your Alpha?"

Finally something where he could completely reassure her. "You might have noticed, but I'm kind of outside the rules. Which means, as my mate, so are you." He pulled her into his arms for a reassuring hug. "No one needs to know the details. If I share that I know that Porter is out of the picture, I won't need to explain any further. I will use my contacts, though, to make sure Porter's car and body are never found. If that's okay?"

Her face was white, the relief pouring off her nearly tangible. "Thank you."

She disappeared back into his bedroom. Blue plopped onto the couch as his legs simply gave way.

Holy. Shit.

Our mate is amazing.

She really is, Furry Blue, Blue agreed.

His wolf all but sniffed with disdain. *You humans spend far too much energy naming things.*

It makes it easier. I can differentiate between my excellent opinions and FB's bullshit opinions, Blue argued before collapsing back, arms spread wide, staring at the ceiling in disbelief. *Great. Now I'm really talking to myself.*

I'm in the same boat, his wolf complained. *And of the two of us, I'm far less likely to bullshit.*

The rest of the evening passed in sweet companionship and more lovemaking. Neither Blue nor his wolf pushed for Steph to accept him completely, though. Sure, she'd shared the secret she had worried he'd accidentally discover. But that didn't mean she was truly ready to dive in, all out.

The next few days made it clear that was the right choice. Steph slowly grew more confident. More *solid* in a way, as if she was truly accepting that they were mates and that she was worthy of being loved by everyone around her.

For the rest of it, not much changed. Blue slipped into her room at the Lodge at night, or Stephanie joined him in his cabin. His house was a little too far away at the moment, but he could see them living there full time eventually, and that thought warmed him inside and out.

You know, shifter males are pretty basic, he told his wolf. *I like the idea of Steph in my territory.*

Soon, his wolf said. *And I agree. We can protect her better at the house. Also, her friends will still be close, just not close enough to interrupt when I am getting a brushing.*

You're spoiled rotten.

But Blue enjoyed the times Steph spent with his wolf side as well. She obviously wasn't frightened, which was great. The weird bit of his wolf talking on the sly with

Stephanie continued. Blue figured out he could hear when it happened—like the faintest of buzzing at the back of his brain—but he never had a clue what was being said.

Jace caught him coming down the stairs Wednesday morning. His cousin motioned him to the side of the front foyer. One of the rare moments that there seemed to be no one else up and about in the lodge yet.

Steph was still snoring. A cute humming sound she made whenever he'd worked her over good, which meant she'd been making it often.

Jace snickered. "I won't bother to ask how you are. The grin and the scent of sex tell me enough."

"You look in a mirror lately?" Blue teased.

"Yeah. We got it pretty damn good, don't we?" Then Jace's expression tightened. "I'm following up on that not really a conversation we had a few days ago. Are you sure that Porter is out of the picture? Your Omega or whatever magic you used to find that out is absolutely certain?"

"My Omega whatever is positive." It wasn't a lie. However their mating finally landed, Steph would take his position title in the pack. Thus, *his Omega* knew for sure. Blue eyed Jace curiously. "Why?"

Jace made a face. "Dwight. We've got that twenty-four/seven watch on him. He's still staying in the cabin, and nothing suspicious has happened. In fact, if anything, he's too damn *not* suspicious."

Interesting. "Like?"

"Nothing but tourist activities. The gondola, the shops on Main Street. He paddled a damn canoe for three hours. Oh, excuse me, two hours and fifty-seven minutes. He didn't want to get charged for overtime."

"He sounds dangerous. Not," Blue agreed. "Time for a direct approach?"

Jace nodded. "I think Del and Angie should accidentally run into him since the law firm was where he emailed in the first place."

"Works for me." Blue considered, remembering the gun Porter had planned to use. "Make sure they have backup in wolf form and the meet happens away from civilians."

His Alpha's expression said all too clearly he knew Blue was keeping secrets. But he simply nodded. "Fine."

A sudden knock hit the massive front door of the lodge.

"Coming," a voice called from both the stairs and the kitchen area.

"Beat you both." Blue chuckled as a tousled Steph and a very pink-cheeked Sophie appeared. He stopped laughing as he swung open the door to reveal a man he recognized instantly by scent.

François.

Good looking, with a neatly trimmed grey-laced beard and moustache. He held a massive bouquet of flowers that he reached toward Stephanie with a suave smile.

Blue growled. Jace growled.

Steph growled.

All three men turned to stare at her, François stood frozen with his arm fully extended.

The cougar shifter took a deep breath. His eyes widened, gaze darting between Stephanie and Blue as the flowers tipped toward the floor. "Well, *merde.*"

A laughing Dixie raced into the foyer, clapping her hands with delight. "Oh. Pretty flowers."

The cat pulled himself together with shocking speed, which was a good thing. Blue didn't really feel like ripping off limbs today. "Which means they're for the prettiest girl in the room." He caught Sophie's eyes quickly, and when she nodded, he presented the bouquet with a flourish to Dixie. "For you, *ma petite*. To celebrate your new family."

"Thank you," she replied sweetly. She kissed his cheek wetly then squealed as she nearly disappeared under the massive bouquet. "Mama, look what the kitty cat gave me."

François sniffed, pulling himself up elegantly. "Kitty cat. *Really.*"

Steph settled into Blue's arms, hand resting on his chest in a familiar petting move. A position that would also make it tough to grab the cat by the throat. "François. Thank you for coming over. Would you like to see where we've placed your art?"

No mention of his wooing gifts. Brilliant woman. Easy, and it allowed the man to pretend none of it had ever happened.

Blue was still very happy when the door closed on the kitty cat's backside an hour later.

Once he'd driven away in his expensive car, Steph pulled Blue to their favourite chairs on the deck.

"Nice growl," he told her. "I adore you."

Steph let her happiness shine out in her ear-to-ear grin. "FB says you wanted to take François apart, which wasn't a good idea. And I didn't want Jace to do it either."

"You were perfect." He muttered to his wolf in his head, *tattletale.*

Steph got that look in her eyes. The one that said FB was talking to her. She snorted then met Blue's gaze. "FB says he also wanted to rip the scruffy feline into pieces. Not that I didn't suspect that was the case."

Blue sighed. "Well, I'm glad that's dealt with."

His mate stared at him suspiciously. "Okay. *Now* what's wrong?"

Shit. He narrowed his eyes. "Are you Omega-ing me?"

"I'm mates-in-training you," she returned. "Spit it out, Blue."

"Furry Blue." Then he cursed. "You really do have that Omega spill-your-secrets-now touch down pat."

Steph slipped onto the deck, settling between his knees, hands on his thighs. "Hate to tell you, but I've always had it. It's the Reiki and massage and the setting of intentions I've spent years learning about. It's just listening hard." She stroked his cheek. "Tell me," she whispered.

"Furry Blue being weirdly separate from me is more than a little uncomfortable," he admitted. When her eyes widened with worry, he hurried to assure her. "Not the part where you're getting to talk to my wolf. And it's not as if it hurts physically or anything."

That little boy inside him who had once been hurt by well-meaning people trying to protect him stepped forward and gave him a nudge, and that in itself was Freudian to the core. His complaint was going to sound so damn childish.

Tell her, his wolf ordered.

Or you will? Blue asked himself, bizarre as the conversation was.

It's your story, his wolf insisted. *It's what makes you, you, remember?* Then he ruined the comforting sentiment by adding, *also, I'm not the one traumatized by trivial human events.*

You're such an ass.

We're such an ass, his wolf restated with amazing self-awareness.

Blue focused on Stephanie to discover a confused expression in her eyes but amusement curling her lips. "What did FB tell you?" he demanded, really getting tired of asking the impossible question.

"That you two were having a meeting of the minds and

once he'd talked sense into you, you'd be back." She stroked her fingers over his face, examining him carefully. "But I don't want you to cave into peer pressure. Not even from yourself."

Blue snickered. "I'm a handful. Trouble every time."

She rose on her knees and pressed a kiss to his lips. Fleeting, but possessive. "It appears that all of you are *my* trouble, though. Talk to me?"

He curled his arms around her. "I'm jealous that I'm not in the mix when you two share secrets. But I don't want you not to share, because you need that safe space. If you can talk to my other side, you're still talking to someone who loves you, so how can I be upset about that?"

"Because feelings don't have to make sense to be real," Steph said quietly. "Also, this whole only *you* or only *FB* talking to me, when it's really *you* and *you* talking to me... That's not normal, Blue. Don't try to pretend that it is and that you have all the answers."

"I won't. Which is why no matter how silly I feel complaining, I'm telling you what's on my mind." He rearranged her so they were face to face with her straddling his lap. "Do not stop talking with Furry Blue to save me some discomfort."

"Don't keep your discomfort to yourself and let me pet you all better." Steph draped her arms over his shoulders. "We're in this together, right?"

"No matter how much we're bullshitting our way through, yes."

They sat there, foreheads touching. Quiet, yet together. Another point of connection. Another step in their journey.

"Get a room," Del called as he pounded up the stairs, grinning at them.

"Great idea." Blue stood. He flipped Steph into

piggyback position, both of them snickering by the time he was done. "Hold on tight," he ordered.

Then he sprinted around Timberwolf Lodge to his on-site cabin and proceeded to enjoy more time with his mate.

IT WAS midafternoon before they finished the ravishing, their lunch break, and another round of ravishing.

"We really need to join the rest of them today." Stephanie ducked out of Blue's reach. "Which means you need to let me put some clothes on."

"They're all shifters. Naked is fine." Blue paused. "Wait. You're right. Cover up now."

He threw his bright pink-and-red lumberjack shirt at her, and she laughed as she pulled it on. "You just realized that if I'm naked, everyone else can see as well. Yes?"

"Yes," he mumbled, hopping into his own clothes. They were scattered all over the floor where they'd fallen in their most recent scramble to get naked.

"They all have mates of their own," Stephanie pointed out.

Blue raised a brow. "Don't try to logic your way out of this. Wear my shirt. It makes me happy."

Which was a good enough reason for many things, Stephanie decided as she walked hand in hand with Blue toward the lodge.

A group had gathered by the firepit—their unofficial clubhouse, it appeared. Steph's friends were setting up a table with refreshments and supper prep. The guys were carrying over firewood to restock the pile. The kids were running in circles around Marvin, who had apparently been taken off childcare duties, because he'd shifted back to his moose form and was patiently waiting for Dixie to climb off his back.

In other words, it was all the happy chaos Stephanie had grown to know and love.

For some reason, Jace, Del, and Lance were all stomping across the yard shirtless. Blue kissed her quickly then ripped his own shirt off again. "Hold this for me. My brethren have summoned me."

He took off at a sprint to catch up.

She pulled the extra shirt on like a jacket over the rest of her clothes as she joined the ladies. "Nice love bite, Sophie."

The young woman smiled with pride. "Thanks."

"Lance has one on his pec, and he deliberately took off his shirt so the guys would see it." Cassidy pointed to the shirtless quartet en route back with armloads of wood. "Which is why the macho posturing is happening."

Stacy lifted a brow. "I need to up my biting game."

So did Steph. Although...teeth also meant mating. She was getting closer, but—

You can bite us without mating, FB assured her. *We like biting. Bite his ear and Blue will lose it.*

And that was info she both wanted and didn't want. *Please don't tell me sex stuff. Talking to the furry side of Blue is weird enough as it is.*

Silly human. It was said with so much affection Stephanie felt the warmth of it to her toes.

"Auntie Steph?" Blaze tugged on her hand.

She tousled the top of his head. "Yeah, kiddo?"

He leaned in close. "How do you stop a wolf from howling in the dark?"

She considered. "Um, that's a tough one. No idea."

"You turn on the lights." Blaze pointed at her. "Your

face is funny, Auntie Steph. Where's Blue? I've got one for him, too."

"Blue's right here." He knelt to be eye to eye with Blaze. "What's up?"

Blaze frowned as he examined Blue's bare torso, then the other men standing around talking half naked. "Mom says we have to wear clothes because it's nearly winter."

"Your mom's right." Stephanie silently handed over Blue's shirt, and he pulled it on before he raised a brow. "Anything else?"

Her nephew opened his mouth eagerly, then his eyes widened, and he hid behind Blue. "Oh, no. It's *her*."

Stephanie twirled to look in the direction Blaze had been staring.

Blue shot to his feet. "Shit."

Across the lawn, an older woman stepped daintily toward them. She wore a perfect blue suit and held a tiny pearl white clutch in her hand. She wasn't the one causing the problem though. It was the young woman boldly walking beside her who had everyone in the group cursing.

"She's not supposed to be here," Stephanie muttered to Blue, still looking at Emma, who had been banished just over a month ago after trying to kill all of them.

Stacy tucked her sons behind her then stepped forward. "Emma Wilson. What are you doing here?" she demanded, deep power in the tone.

It was probably something that Jace should've asked, but Stacy had some precedent, considering she was the one who put the last hurt on Emma.

Instead of Emma answering, the older woman held up a hand. "My apologies, Alphas of the Jasper pack. Considering I've been granted the authority to decide the final destiny of the Timberwolf Lodge, I hoped you'd consider a discussion."

She spoke haughtily. Regally, even. As if walking onto someone else's territory with an outcast was peachy keen and no problem. The protectors of the pack had all moved into defensive positions.

Wait. Authority to *decide*...

The Wilson Pack. *This* was who got to say if they kept Timberwolf Lodge?

Stephanie glanced at Blue, but he was staring intently at Emma as if trying to read her mind.

Jace nodded slowly. "You are welcome, Ermeline." He lifted a finger and pointed at Emma. "But that one was warned that the next time she stepped into our territory, her life was forfeit."

"Unless invited to return by the pack Omega." Emma grinned at Blue. "Which my niece tells me happened on the night of the teen event. Thanks *so* much for issuing an open invitation for *all* of Carolyn's relatives to come visit anytime they wanted."

Slightly ahead of Stephanie, Blue's shoulders stiffened, then he cursed under his breath.

"Did you make that offer?" Jace asked quietly.

"I might have. I was only being polite, though. It shouldn't have been enough to allow an outcast safe passage."

Jace nodded and focused his attention on their visitors. "To what end do we deserve this unexpected surprise?"

Ermeline took another assessing peek at the lodge. "Being here the other day reminded me of the times when we used to have all sorts of challenges set up at Timberwolf Lodge. Your Auntie Rachel and Uncle Jim hosted fantastic events. I wondered if you planned on doing anything like that again this year. It's too late for a fall festival, but perhaps a winter one?"

Cassidy now stood beside Jace, arms folded over her chest. "We have some ideas."

For the first time, a crack showed in Ermeline's exterior. A hint of cunning and mischief. The emotion was gone before Stephanie could confirm it had been there. "I adore the entertainment of a real wolf event. The challenges, the creativity—"

"The fights to the death," Emma added casually before batting her lashes sweetly at Stacy. "Good to see you again. How's your sweet little boy? Think he'd like to play hide and seek with me?" She peered behind Stacy and attempted to make eye contact with Ace. She'd used him before in a mad attempt to take over the lodge.

"Try it, and you'll get more than a bite and a scratch this time." Stacy said it calmly, but there was ice in her tone.

"Bitch." Emma sneered, showing her teeth. "You won't fucking touch me. You wouldn't have had the guts or the strength to follow through in the first place."

Surprisingly, Ermeline spoke up instantly to scold her niece. "Stop that. Civilized wolves show their superiority in a challenge, not with nasty words and a bad attitude. Really, I'd have thought you'd have learned that by now, Emma. I'm ashamed I have to remind one of my offspring of such a simple rule."

Emma flushed, her embarrassment feeding her anger. But she meekly replied, "Yes, Auntie."

The older wolf's gaze drifted over the entire group, hesitated on Blue, then landed back on Cassidy. "I would find it entertaining if you ran a small event this year. A way for your wolves to show their true strength."

"And is this important for the positive conclusion of our challenge to win Timberwolf Lodge?" Cassidy asked.

Ermeline shrugged. "A challenge is always a good way to find out who's deserving of treasures."

Emma twisted on the spot to grin at her auntie. "I want to compete. I want to compete so I can prove that *I'm* the most deserving."

The old woman glared at her, somehow never losing her superior air. "For someone who's not supposed to be here, you assume many things. Including my interest in what *you* want. Now be *silent*."

But Emma plowed right ahead. "But, Auntie, you always say that the wolf who can't protect their land shouldn't be allowed to keep it. So why not the oldest of challenges? Plus, here on Timberwolf land, it would only be right to have a challenge between the Jasper pack and the Wilsons."

A hush slid over the gathered wolves. Uneasy. Unsettled.

"What's the oldest challenge?" Stacy asked quietly. "For us not in the know."

"A variation on Capture The Flag. One group of three defends, the other attacks. At the end of the day, whoever has won will be clear." Emma placed a hand delicately on her aunt's arm. "Honorable wolves often use this challenge to prove their worth and move up in the pack, since no leadership members are allowed to compete."

Cassidy leaned toward Stephanie and whispered. "Jace doesn't like it."

"Do we have a choice?" Stephanie whispered back. "Ermeline decides whether we get to keep Timberwolf Lodge or not."

"It's a risk."

"Is there a way out of it?"

"Not really."

Blue had been staring intently at Jace. He nodded, then stepped forward. "We accept the challenge. I'll captain the Timberwolf team."

"You don't get to choose." Emma all but danced as she said the words. "I made the challenge, you accepted. Now *I* pick my opponent."

A deep growl rose from the gathered wolves. All except Ermeline, who looked slightly bored by the details.

She shrugged. "Complain all you want, but Emma is right. Annoying, but right. Emma, claim your opponent. The challenge is set for tomorrow morning, starting at nine. Who do you call from the Jasper pack, Emma Wilson?"

Emma no longer looked drug-soaked, but the madness was still there in her eyes. She stepped forward and pointed, delight written on her expression.

"Stephanie Nix."

17

Emma's voice rang with the sound of triumph as fear flooded Stephanie's belly as if a dam had burst. Accepting a challenge from a wolf with murderous tendencies screamed bad idea.

Careful, FB warned. *You are* pack, *so she can choose you. She thinks she's being smart, but she doesn't know you like we do.*

Clearly, the dangerous wolf had expected Stephanie to turn down the challenge. Possibly this was a layer of deception. If she had shouted a denial, would that have meant an immediate win for Emma?

Thanks for the warning. What do I do next?

Tell her you accept. Wait— He paused. *Tell her if the challenge is skill to skill, you accept.*

She didn't ask for clarification. Stephanie ignored Emma completely, speaking directly to the older woman who was the only reason any of this nonsense had value. "Skill to skill?"

Ermeline's lips twitched. "Of course."

Beside her, Emma looked furious, but she nodded. "Agreed."

Good. Now accept, then kick them out. The less Emma knows about what comes next, the better. FB's voice was accompanied by the sensation of a hand slipping into hers. Blue joining her, standing strong and tall by her side.

"Challenge accepted. If you'd please leave now. Lance will accompany you."

She didn't bother with any other niceties, and if Emma sneered the entire way off Timberwolf land, Stephanie didn't give a hoot.

Instead, she twisted to face Blue and focused on him until it was clear by the rest of the pack surrounding them that they were back to friends only. "So. I guess I get to play some werewolf games."

"That was brilliant." Blue examined her closely. "FB told you about the skill to skill part?"

Stephanie nodded. "Now explain. I just followed his instructions."

He snorted. "You're amazing. It means anyone who meets face to face can only fight with their greatest common asset. So you won't fight Emma or her team if they're in wolf form. Only human, and no weapons."

It was better than worrying about being clawed to ribbons by a furious Emma wolf. "I can do that."

"You'll do great." This from Jace. When she met his gaze, he nodded. "I mean it. Don't let the idea of the challenge get in your head. This isn't like when Del and I went up against each other."

"No, because Stephanie has more brains in her little finger than the two of you combined." Cassidy slid in close. "You can do this. I know you can. We just need to find you two amazing partners."

"I'm one of them," Blue said, his grip on her hand firm and steady. "Neither Jace nor Del can offer since leadership is excluded from the challenge. Only I'm an Omega..."

"You're outside the leadership rules." Impossible that she could laugh at a time like this. "Dear, sweet Blue. Always the rule breaker, aren't you?"

"For you? Forever."

"You're in," she confirmed as she considered the rest of the people gathered. She was going up against wolf shifters to protect Timberwolf Lodge. Jace was out, Del was out. Lance was a possibility...

Don't think like a wolf. Consider your options. What's your intention, and who can best help you meet that need?

This time, it wasn't FB in her head. It was every training video and class she'd ever taken about trusting her intuition to find the right path forward.

The instant she saw it she knew. "Pack members only for the challenge, right? Who's considered pack?"

Everyone around her considered carefully.

"Wolves born into the pack," Sophie said.

Cassidy pointed around the circle at the couples represented. "Mates."

Del considered. "The last group I can think of are the ones accepted as family. Some because they've been friends for years, some because they care for the very old or the very young."

Perfect. Stephanie gave a sharp whistle, and Marvin lifted his massive moose head from where he'd been munching on rushes by the side of the lake. "Hey, Marvin. You got time tomorrow to help me defend the castle from a maniacal drug-infected wolf with delusions of grandeur?"

Marvin considered for a moment then dipped his chin, his ginormous racks swaying eight feet in the air.

Stephanie turned back to her friends and family. *Her pack.* "I have a team. Now someone please tell me the rest of the rules, because while I don't mind breaking them, I'd like to know what I'm jumping into before I get anyone else hurt."

~

SHE WAS AMAZING. The entire time Jace and Del went over rules and strategy, Stephanie stayed alert and asked damn good questions. She also filled half of a notebook with scrawled notes and teeny quick sketches, which had Blue shaking his head.

"You're not going to be able to see what you've written," he warned.

"I don't have to. Writing it down helps me to remember it." She stuck out her tongue. "Now hush. The big bad wolves are teaching me stuff."

"We're learning just as much from you," Del said smoothly. "Picking Marvin as your third? Brilliant. Emma won't see that coming."

"Emma will see him the instant she steps anywhere onto the open lawn around the lodge. I don't give her high odds of surviving a direct confrontation with the lodge moose." Cassidy high-fived Steph.

Del was right. Jace, Del and Blue had thought they'd be finding ways to keep Steph safe, when she just kept coming up with one fantastic idea after another.

"Let's see if I've got it covered." Stephanie pointed to sections of her notebook. "Emma's team will not approach the lodge from anywhere except the lawn and lake side, because the rest of you are going to hold an enormous party all day long in the parking lot."

"We can't keep her out, but we can shout if anyone shows up," Cassidy agreed.

"A shout of *Happy Birthday* is not against the rules. And I'd just have to come see what was going on, then, wouldn't I? Since I love cake and all." Marvin sat in his usual rocking chair.

He didn't seem to be paying much attention, except Blue knew the man. He was a rock-solid final backup plan. Considering moose could run as fast as a wolf and nearly double the speed of a human, he was a great guard as a final line of defense.

No lone wolf would willingly come near a moose. They were a death sentence on hooves.

Steph nodded firmly, still checking her notes. "Blue and I will work the rest of the perimeter. At some point Emma's going to try to slip in, but we'll try to spot her first. We'll check the treehouse, the boathouse, and the lookout tower. Otherwise, we keep moving in a circle along the perimeter. If we do spot her, we ignore stealth and make as much noise as possible. Pin her down and wait for the timer to end."

"Blue's sniffer is excellent, so don't ignore his warnings," Del reminded her.

"Got it. An A-class sniffer." She winked at Blue. "You need a certificate or something."

"Or something," he agreed. "Enough talk. It's time to rest. Tomorrow will come soon enough, and Steph needs to be ready."

It still took a long time to break apart and head in different directions. Steph stopped and spoke with her sister and Cassidy privately for a good long time.

While he waited, Blue's friends surrounded him.

Del eyed him, amusement on his face.

"What?"

Their Alpha-turned-Enforcer shrugged. "A year ago, if someone had said you'd be involved in a wolf challenge with a human and a moose by your side, I wouldn't have believed it. Not because you don't have the skills, but because it's not...*you*."

"We all have to grow up sometime." Blue raised a brow. "And besides, it's not me with them by my side. I'm in a challenge beside Steph. She's the center. She's the reason."

"On that note—you're going to take care of Steph, got that?" Jace had that glowing Alpha look in his eyes.

"Already planned on it," Blue offered dryly.

"No, I mean if things get dangerous, get her out of there. I know it's skill to skill, but accidents can happen. If the girls lose the lodge, they'll survive. If they lose Steph, they'll never get over it."

Del nodded. "Agreed. Stephanie is their heart. No matter how much they love the lodge, it's not worth her dying over."

"No arguments from me." Blue accepted solid hugs from his friends. The back pounding was especially vigorous tonight, and his Omega sense kicked into high gear for long enough to know both Jace and Del were worried, but they trusted Blue absolutely. Which was both an ego stroke and an affirming kick in the butt. He had an important job to do tomorrow.

Tonight? He had a different important task.

She's ready, his wolf told him.

Thanks, FB. Blue turned with his hand outstretched and caught her to his side. "Thanks everyone. We'll see you in the morning for breakfast."

Stephanie's fingers in his were cool, but she held on tightly. Silently, they crossed the distance between the firepit and the cabin he'd claimed.

"Let's sit on the deck for a bit," Steph requested.

"It's getting colder," Blue warned.

"We'll cuddle. I'll grab a blanket."

She vanished inside.

I need time with Steph. His wolf said it quietly. *You'll have the rest of the night with her. I want now.*

How could Blue argue with that? He stripped and shifted, jumping up on to the loveseat to wait for her return.

The surprise in her eyes was there, but she settled beside him. "Hey. You need a cuddle as well?"

The next hour ranked up there with the strangest Blue had ever experienced. Stephanie and his wolf chatted, and while he felt it happening, Blue couldn't hear the actual words. Emotions drifted through the weird veil between his selves—a strong sense of love with the occasional burst of amusement.

The only clear part was Stephanie's fingers stroking his fur, and Blue finally gave up fighting to hear what was going on and focused on the tactile pleasure of her touch.

When his wolf side retreated, giving up control, Blue shifted and stretched. His wolf in strange rebellion, his mate facing danger, their mate bond still not complete... A sense of wellbeing surrounded Blue beyond what he should feel, all things considered.

Especially when Stephanie stepped against him, all warm and soft and...*naked?*

He glanced down in surprise. Yup. Her clothes were in a messy pile to the side of the loveseat. Which at least meant he hadn't missed too much. "Um?"

She laughed, soft and sultry. "I'm all talked out for now. Time for a different kind of conversing."

The cold fall air swirled into the cabin with them, but damn if he cared. Naked Stephanie ranked up there in his top ten things on earth. "I can do that. My tongue needs some exercise."

"Blue." She sounded scandalized, and her cheeks were flushed. But maybe that was from the cold.

He should check. Other parts of her should be flushed if it was the cold.

He caught her around the thighs and lifted her skyward. Steph clutched his head, laughing as he brought her inside and tossed her on the bed. "I'm not a sack of potatoes," she complained.

"Nope. You're a sack of sugar."

"Really? What—? Oh, yes. *Dammit*, Blue. I wanted to—"

Her protests died away as he danced his tongue over her skin. He kissed her mouth, her neck. Over her breasts and all the way to between her legs. Teasing her entrance with his fingers and kissing her everywhere until she squirmed with pleasure.

Only then did he notch his cock to her pussy and slide in.

One. Inch. At. A. Time.

The entire time he stared into her eyes. Their blue depths were filled with happiness and pleasure, and that alone sent streaks of need racing through him.

"Blue?"

"Yeah?" He had pressed in fully, groins locked together like a sensual human jigsaw puzzle. Her leg over his hip, arms tangled, mouths coming together in a heated kiss.

When he let her breathe, Steph sucked for air then spoke, softly but firmly. "I love you."

She'd said it first this time.

Blue squeezed his eyes together and let the rush of emotion tangling over them grow bigger and bigger.

Tangible heat, all of it teasingly good on the skin. Their love a living, breathing thing wrapping them in a cocoon.

He opened his eyes and found her grinning at him. Moving together with a rhythm that needed no other music.

"I love you too," he shared as pleasure streaked up his spine.

Steph moaned. "Oh, *Blue.*"

Shooting stars. Fireworks. Northern lights. None of them compared with the wild energy flying around the small cabin as they hit the peak and fell together.

Fell into love.

LAST NIGHT's warmth seemed far away.

"How the hell is there snow on the ground?" Stephanie demanded of her sister, glaring at the lawn that had been green yesterday but was now an endless field of white.

They'd had a good breakfast—not that Stephanie had eaten much, considering her nerves. She'd dressed warmly with boots and mitts to deal with the unexpected snow. Now all her team were getting last minute good wishes and instructions from their friends.

It was ten minutes and counting until nine a.m. and the start of the challenge. Ermeline had shown up to be an official witness. She sat on the back deck that overlooked the lake, a pot of tea before her and a haughty expression on her face.

Sophie and Lance were chatting with Marvin, who was already in moose form. Jace, Del, and Cassidy were with Blue. And Stephanie had her sister for a sweet final chat.

"Welcome to winter in Jasper." Stacy laid a hand on

Steph's arm. "According to Colt, his wolf says the snow will help you."

"Track, yes. Stay warm and dry? Highly unlikely." Stephanie squared her shoulders. "Ugh. Fine. Girding my loins for a miserable twelve hours."

"You're a nut."

Stephanie found herself being squeezed tightly. "Um, thanks?"

Stacy set her partially free. She held onto Steph's hands and met her gaze intently. "You're pretending to be all complaining and *oh, woe is me*, but I know you, sis. It's all a show. Like always, you're solidly there for us. You're a rock, and I haven't said often enough how grateful I am for everything you've done for me and the kids over the years. I haven't said often enough how much I love you."

Damn it. "You're going to make me cry," Stephanie warned. "I get all spotty and mottled when I cry, and won't that make a wonderful team photo at the start of this madcap event?"

Stacy hugged and kissed her one last time. "That's from me and Cassidy and all the boys. And Del and Jace and Sophie and Jessica and everyone else here at the lodge. We love you, and we trust you, but no matter what, you stay safe and come back in one piece. Got it?"

"Yes, Mom." Stacy's eyeroll was exactly what Stephanie needed. "I'll do my best on all those things."

There were no long farewells. Two minutes before the top of the hour, those staying behind moved in two directions. Cassidy went to sit with Ermeline, and the rest headed to the south side of the lodge to begin their all day long *just casually hanging out in the parking lot* party.

Marvin slowly wandered to a spot in the middle of the

lawn. His massive hoof prints stood out clearly in the unbroken snow.

Blue saluted him then waited for Stephanie to join him at the perimeter of the trees. "Ready? You look well dressed."

"Like a turkey," she agreed with amusement.

His eyes danced. "Good to see you're feeling chipper this morning."

"Not much else I can do," she pointed out. "Rock and hard place—but if I have to do this, I'm glad I get to do this with you."

He squeezed her shoulders then turned her toward the path. "Let's start our search."

There should have been a starters' gun. Or a band. Nope. Nothing except the quiet sounds of the forest on a cold wintery day.

Stephanie took a step forward and it began.

The first hour passed quickly enough. The snow hadn't had time to accumulate, and the wind had died down. Which meant they left tracks, but it wasn't enough to turn the weather freezing or make walking uncomfortable.

Second hour of exploring copied the first. They walked in silence, Stephanie listening as hard as she could. A few steps away from her, Blue was inhaling hard enough to hyperventilate, but so far he hadn't scented anything.

They stopped every half hour to have a sip of water and few bites of food. She wasn't hungry but knew she needed to keep her energy up. It was going to be a long afternoon and evening.

It was nearly two o'clock when they discovered tracks.

"One in wolf, two in human," Blue said quietly, pointing at where Emma's party had topped the ridge.

Stephanie followed the line of tracks farther to the north. "They split up."

Blue swore softly.

She knew exactly what was wrong. The wolf had gone on his own. "We have to follow them."

"I don't want to leave you with two to follow." He squeezed her hand tightly, the layers of mittens between them keeping his warmth from her. "I'll shift. Hopefully I catch up with this one and deal with them quickly. I'll come back to help you as soon as I can."

"That makes sense. Let's not talk about it; let's just do it." She caught him, though, holding onto his face and pulling him in for a quick, intense kiss. "You stay safe," she ordered. "I mean it."

Blue pulled off his clothes and she stuffed the pile into her backpack. "Yes, Captain."

He shifted. His white wolf camouflaged beautifully with the white around them. At least there was that in their favor.

He took off running, vanishing down the trail the other wolf had left.

Stephanie was alone.

The sky overhead was grey and bleak, colder temperatures sliding in as if rolling down the side of the mountain. Such a pretty day for a walk in the forest. *Not.*

When the snow started to fall again, Stephanie flipped a mental bird at the weather gods and kept going.

The trail was easy to follow. Stephanie did her best to be a smart tracker and figure out what was going on from the tracks before her. One of them looked as if the walker kept losing their balance, toe scuffs and skid marks more than a clear one foot after another.

Her thighs burned as she made her way up a short, steep section. Her head popped over the top and she froze, the sight of a small shack not even twenty feet away making her heart pound. It wasn't in very good shape, but it also wasn't one of the buildings they had discussed having to examine.

Only a five-minute walk from the far north side of the lake. Stephanie wondered why she'd never seen the place before.

Motion blurred at the edge of her peripheral vision. She whirled to find Emma bearing down at her at a full sprint, a large club-like object in her hand.

So much for the skill to skill, no weapons part. It didn't seem like the time to try and debate the rules with Emma now, though. Not while Stephanie was unarmed.

She ran.

A clear trail led downward, and somewhere close by there was a clearing. That much she knew because when they played disc golf, one of her favorite holes had a basket on this side of the lake.

What's wrong? It was FB, loud and clear. Which said nothing about how close Blue was but still, hope rose.

Emma is chasing me, she told FB. *Headed down the hill to basket eight.*

I'm coming. Will be there shortly, he promised.

Stephanie ducked under another outstretched spruce limb then slid over the crest of a hill and into the clearing. *Emma's cheating. She's got a weapon of sorts.*

Cheat back.

Emma was hard on her heels. "Don't run away little girl. I have something for you."

Gah. "You're annoying and condescending." Stephanie pulled to a stop on the other side of the basket, feeling a little safer with the sturdy metal contraption between the two of them. "Emma. Nice baseball bat."

The other woman grinned. "Sports can teach us so much."

Truth. Which is why Stephanie was very grateful that her nephews had not followed instructions to put away their equipment. She scooped into the bottom of the wire basket and snatched up the discs that had been left there.

She backed up just far enough to pack a punch, pulled back her arm, and then sent one of the discs flying directly into Emma's face.

She heard the strike land, but Stephanie was already on the move back the way she had come. *I'm headed toward a small cabin. Just to the north of the basket,* she told FB.

Nearly there.

Stephanie hit the top of one section of the trail, turned, and threw again, this time a forehand shot, which meant she saw the disc hit. It was very satisfying to watch Emma's face turn bright red with anger, the white line where the disc had hit her forehead showing up in stark contrast.

Not enough time to truly enjoy it, Stephanie was off and running again, fighting to keep her own balance as she jumped over and under brush. The shack grew closer. Closer still.

Emma's steady stream of curses and hot angry panting grew closer as well.

Stephanie could have sworn she felt hot breath on the back of her neck as she pushed open the door and scurried inside. She scrambled to shut the door behind her, fingernails dragging over the doorframe in search of a bolt to throw even as she leaned into the door.

Emma hit the door with her full body weight, and the

wooden slab opened slightly before Stephanie forced it closed, threw the latch, and breathed a sigh of relief.

I'm in the shack, she warned FB. *Emma's outside, smacking the door with a bat. Be careful.*

Stephanie turned...and froze.

It was a horrifying flashback to years earlier. The lone window let in a pitiful amount of light but enough to show she was out of the frying pan and into the fire.

Porter—no, *Dwight*—stood in the grey-washed shadows a few feet away. His face was twisted in anger and the gun in his hand pointed straight at Stephanie's belly.

18

$\mathcal{A}$ haze floated over Stephanie's eyes, and she fought to stay motionless. "Dwight."

He blinked hard, gun hand wavering. Not enough to move the business end away from her, but enough to show he wasn't fully in control of what he was doing.

Which seemed more dangerous in some ways than less.

He didn't speak. Just stood there with the gun on her and panic in his eyes. Rather terrifying, but it also gave her time to look him over a little more closely.

Dwight was not in good shape. He was the one who had been nearly falling on the hike through the woods. His face was bruised, and a trickle of blood ran down his temple. His hands were dirty and his knuckles skinned. Not as if he'd been hitting someone, but as if he'd been trying to defend himself.

Outside the shed, Blue had arrived. The banging on the door stopped, and snarls and growling mixed with Emma's cursed shouts.

Dwight shivered then braced himself, adjusting his grip

on the gun and focusing harder on Stephanie. "I won't let you kill me."

Okaaaay. "I don't want to kill you. Nobody wants to kill you," she said softly.

He flicked his chin upward as if pointing to outside. "She told me what you planned. How the monsters act—what they'll do because I know about them."

Emma had told him...*what?* "Can you aim that gun somewhere away from me while we talk about this? Because there are no monsters who plan to kill you. I'm as human as you, swear to God on a stack of bibles."

Dwight considered then tilted his head toward the corner of the shack. "Sit there. Put your hands behind you and sit in the corner, and then I'll take the gun off you. But I'll shoot if you attack."

"If that makes you feel better, fine by me." Stephanie hurried to the corner and sat, hands behind her. She pressed her shoulders firmly against the log wall. Which really wasn't as bad of a position as he might have thought considering she was damn flexible and spry.

As long as the tip of that gun was now pointed at the floor instead of her, Stephanie was happy.

Especially when the volume from Emma and Blue's fight rose again. Emma must have shifted to wolf, because there were now two snarling beasts outside the door.

Dwight's face was completely white. "They're fighting each other? If you're human, what are we going to do?"

"What did Emma tell you?" Stephanie repeated gently. "And are you okay? Who hurt you?"

"I was kidnapped. I came here on my vacation, and yes there was some nonsense about people who could turn into wolves, but I was mostly here for a holiday. Last night somebody came into my cabin and beat me up. They blindfolded me and put me in the trunk of a car. This morning Emma rescued me. She told me that the people who kidnapped me were monsters, and she was going to try to save me. If anybody else came in the shack, I needed to shoot first and ask questions later."

Thank goodness for small mercies. "I'm really glad you didn't shoot me," Stephanie said honestly. "And there is a lot I need to tell you, but you need to trust me. Yes, there are what some people would consider monsters, but Emma is at the top of that list."

His hand was shaking again. He hadn't aimed the gun at her again, but his head twisted from side to side, and he looked on the verge of tears. "I didn't want this. I didn't want any of this. I was just trying to find my brother, and then everything went out of control."

Boy, did she ever have a lot of sympathy for this man. Because if what he was saying was true, he'd been dropped into the wonderful world of wolves with even less warning than she, Cassidy, and her sister had.

Because honestly, a cute little wolf pup landing in your hands is different than the snarling beasts fighting outside the door of a shed.

Stephanie closed her eyes. Stupid maybe, but it seemed like the thing to do. She took a deep breath in and thought about her intentions. Thought about what would make this moment better, what poor Dwight needed to be able to deal with the shock and mistreatment.

A calm, cool springtime breeze sensation swirled around her. She took another deep breath and let it out. And another.

When an enormous sigh came from the other side of the room, she opened her eyes to discover Dwight standing with his gun arm completely relaxed by his side.

He gaped at her with wonder and confusion. "What did you just do?"

She shrugged softly. "Adjusted our chakras? I'm not one hundred percent sure, but this much I know. You're not in danger anymore. I promise you that, and while there are things that go bump in the night, the people I know will do everything to keep you safe. Okay?"

He shook his head slightly from side to side, but when he spoke it was in awe and not denial. "I don't know what you're doing, but I trust you."

Dwight leaned down and placed the gun on the ground, backing away from it as if offering it to her.

Stephanie made a face as she got to her feet. "Do you know how to use that?"

Dwight shook his head. "Pull the trigger?"

Okay dokey. "I know how, but I'm not a fan. You okay if I pick it up?" she double-checked.

A quick nod. Dwight seemed to be listening hard. "They're gone. What was fighting outside the door?"

"Wolves," she told him simply as she carefully handled the gun. "One second."

She tried peering out the window, but it faced toward the lake and the fighting had been to the south of the cabin.

Where are you? she asked FB.

Chasing the bitch. I made a very good attack, and she chickened out. She's staying to the west of the lodge. Are you safe?

Very safe. I'm headed back to the lodge. Don't get hurt. She's sneaky.

She more sensed than heard FB's pride. *She is slower than she thinks. If she keeps moving in the proper direction, I won't need to run her over.*

Nodding to herself, Stephanie gestured toward the

door. "The wolves are gone for now, so let's get you somewhere safe. I'll tell you what I can, and you can answer some questions I have. Sound all right?"

Dwight pressed a hand to his chest as they walked into the still overcast day, though the contrast was enough to set them both blinking.

"I thought I was going to die in there," he admitted softly.

She patted his back gently. "You're alive, and you'll stay that way," she promised again.

He touched his beaten face tenderly. "Maybe we should hurry to that safe spot?"

Stephanie guided him back down the route she had run away from Emma, straight toward the lodge.

"What were you doing in Jasper?" she asked. "I know you said a vacation, but you also said something about a wolf?"

"First, tell me how you knew my name." Dwight made a face. "I just realized that. You called me by name when you came in the door."

"This part is going to sound like a fairy tale, but we're sort of related. My sister was married to your brother. You look a lot alike."

Dwight swore. "You knew Porter?"

"Yep." Maybe the less said the better.

"That asshole." Dwight walked beside Stephanie now on the level grass at the edge of the lake, headed toward the lodge at a rapid pace. "We weren't close, in case you were wondering."

"I got that idea. We didn't know you existed," she told him. "Not until you sent a letter to a local lawyer. He's now married to my sister, Porter's ex."

"What a tangled mess." Dwight shook his head. "That

letter. Porter and I never really got along, and then we had an incident or two that made me cut all ties with him. The last I heard, he'd gone into the military and that was it for years.

"Then about six months ago, I got a notification to pick up his possessions because the contract he had on a storage unit had expired, and the credit card was out of date. I was listed as next of kin."

"You got Porter's stuff?" God, what had the evil man hidden away?

"Not a ton of stuff. Some of his military things and a bunch of notebooks. I would have chucked the entire thing, only our dad had just died. He'd never updated his will, so the inheritance is in both Porter and my names. I figured I owed it to my dad to at least try to track Porter down. The notebooks were full of crazy talk and angry ideas. And something about a friend in the military who turned into a wolf." Dwight shrugged. "I figured it was drunk talk."

"It's not...but it's also complicated." They were at the edge of the lawn now, Marvin eyeing her with curiosity.

"Holy shit. Don't move." Dwight Tremblant stepped protectively in front of her. "Moose are dangerous, but they don't see very well. Let's back up slowly and go around the other side of that big hotel."

If she had any doubts before this, his protective actions convinced her Dwight was one of the good guys.

She laid a hand on his shoulder. "Remember that bit about there being monsters, but you're safe? I need you to listen and keep trusting me."

~

Blue had a scratch on his nose that stung in the cool air, and a thirst for blood that really wasn't very attractive.

She wanted to hurt our mate, FB said. *No mercy.*

Win the challenge first. Punishment later.

Emma slipped, and Blue was on her. He cuffed her solidly and enjoyed watching her feet skid out from under her. Her body slid on the snowy ground hard enough she smacked into a tree.

Blue lowered his center and growled at her, waiting for her to rise.

She moved slowly, as if deliberately trying to waste time. When she was finally vertical, she darted onto the tree stump beside her, shifted her momentum, and launched straight at him.

Only instead of slamming into him, she soared over his head, landed smoothly, and kept going. Straight down the hill toward the lodge.

Stephanie is going to the lodge, FB informed him.

Shit. Had something happened?

Why? Even as he asked the question, Blue put on his full speed and raced after Emma.

She didn't waver, all her focus straight ahead. She was just enough smaller that she managed to duck under logs that Blue had to go around. It slowed him enough to keep Emma out of reach.

Which meant when they burst out onto the clearing, Blue frantically searched for Marvin as well as Steph.

Emma ignored the potential danger. Now that they were in the clear, Blue had the advantage, and he was suddenly three steps away. Two...

They both skidded to a stop just feet away from Marvin, who was only a few feet away from the deck of the lodge.

Blue shifted, popping up on his human feet like a yo-yo

and taking the steps to where his mate stood. "Steph. What's going on? You okay?"

"I'm fine. We had a discovery, though."

At the table on the deck, Ermeline sat with her arms folded over her chest, her expression unreadable. Cassidy had pulled out a chair beside the matriarch for Dwight, and Stephanie was pouring the man a cup of tea.

Okay. Not the situation Blue had expected. "Are we still involved in the challenge?"

Ermeline raised a brow. "I'm waiting for the answer to that myself."

"We'll get to the challenge in a minute. First things first." Steph ignored Ermeline's sniffle of disapproval and patted Dwight's shoulder instead. "Drink your tea. You need the sugar after a shock. So, like I told you, this is my mate. Yes, he was a wolf a minute ago. And Marvin is the moose, also a shifter. So your brother was right, and there are people who can shift into animals. But being a shifter doesn't mean being bad. On a scale of one to ten, my mate is a two baddie. Your brother, although fully human—sorry about this—was a full scale ten asshole."

Dwight nodded then outright dropped his teacup, scrambling back in the chair when Emma shifted and crawled up on the deck. "She's the one who gave me the gun. She said you would kill me."

Stephanie slid between Dwight and Emma in a flash. "Hey, Emma. Why don't we start with you explaining to your auntie what skill to skill means? Because considering this challenge was supposed to be about *honour*, you either seriously suck at comprehension or you're a massive cheat."

Emma ignored her. Just stared at Dwight. Then a slow, evil smile formed on her lips that made the hair on the back of Blue's neck stand on end.

"Thanks, *teammate*. You appear to have done your job." She bowed slightly to her grandmother. "I think you'd agree that my team member Dwight breeched the lodge defenses. In fact, it looks as if he's fully infiltrated their numbers. Challenge over in my favour."

Stephanie made a rude noise. "You beat up this poor man, told him the next person coming into the shack was going to kill him, and you think me rescuing him makes you a winner?"

Emma shrugged. "Unless you brought him here to use as an example of what happens to your enemies. Tell you what—slit his throat, and you win. I'm okay with that."

Blue snarled the words. "That's not going to happen."

"It's within the rules," Emma snapped back. "Or you can admit defeat. Honour is not always about shredding our enemies, but if it's necessary, we do it. There are three iron-clad rules in the Wilson pack. Defend your property. Power takes over. Keep the upper hand. You've done none of these things today."

The rest of the pack leadership were there by that point. Cassidy had probably used her mate bond to call Jace, and the rest of the group from the parking lot joined them. It was an odd collection of people gathered around the small table where one visiting stranger held court.

"You're right, Emma." The old woman sniffed delicately. "Stephanie? Will one of your team be killing this man?"

"Absolutely not." Stephanie sounded more pissed off than afraid. She slipped her hand into Blue's, the connection between them solid and strong as she spoke for them all. "If that's what's required, for an innocent man's life to end because *Emma* thinks it would be a good game, screw it. Not happening. Not in any pack I'm a part of."

Emma was clearly disappointed that the man hadn't had his throat ripped out in front of them all.

Ermeline, on the other hand, eyed her niece as if she'd just spotted an interesting spot of mold on the wall. "You are the winner of the challenge. Congratulations."

Emma threw her arms in the air and howled, the sound strange emitting from her human throat.

Then she whirled on Jace and Cassidy. "Leave now. Don't touch a thing, just get off my land."

"That's unreasonable—" Cassidy began.

"I could kill you all where you stand for trespassing. Letting you live is so much more civil and humane," Emma pointed out, her expression smarmy as if she were some ungracious, evil hostess. "I've wanted this lodge forever, and now it's mine. I have my own place to create a pack."

"You are so much drama." Ermeline pushed to her feet. She shoved past her niece forcibly enough that Emma fell to the ground. Ermeline stared at Dwight for a moment, then shrugged. "Jace. I trust you have a way to make the problem of him go away? Or Blue? I really don't think we need humans running around town shouting about us. Next thing you know people will be trying to use us for science experiments."

Emma scrambled upright. "What are you talking about? Jace is leaving. Blue is leaving. All of them are leaving."

"Silence." Ermeline didn't shout, but this time instead of volume, she used the power of an Alpha.

Her niece's complaints shut off like a tap had closed.

"I didn't intend to do this so quickly, but since you've been patient, and since your cooperation allowed me to truly dig out the information I needed, I think it's appropriate." Ermeline stepped in front of Cassidy. "I hereby declare the terms of the lottery complete. You have met the approval of the Wilson pack. Timberwolf Lodge is officially yours."

Shocked gasps slipped from all the girls, and Steph's grip on Blue's hand tightened. "I didn't lose the lodge for us?" she asked shakily.

"You were never in a position to lose it," the older woman assured her. She turned her sharp gaze on Emma. "You, on the other hand, are an ungrateful wench. How *dare* you try to go around me?"

"That's not fair. I won the challenge. They did not defend from the enemy, which means I won," Emma roared.

"That's not what the contest was about," the old lady said. "The rules state *I* get to decide if they keep the lodge. The challenge was just a game. You're the one who assumed winning it meant anything more."

Emma turned red then blue. For a second it looked as if she might make a leap at her aunt, but she stood in place, hands flexing as if preparing to release her claws.

Blue braced in case Emma foolishly leapt to attack anyone in his pack.

Jace rose to his feet. "Mrs. Wilson. Thank you for your decision regarding Timberwolf Lodge. But we have a serious matter to deal with. Your niece."

"Exactly right." Ermeline stared harshly at her younger relative. "You have horrendous manners. I should let him discipline you properly."

Emma froze. Discipline in this context meant death.

Cassidy interrupted. "Ermeline, perhaps with your years of experience, you could advise us. Emma was removed from the Jasper pack for dangerous behavior. A casual invite through a younger relative shouldn't have been enough to allow her free rein back onto our territory."

The older woman had the grace to look embarrassed. "That was mostly my fault."

Cassidy frowned.

Ermeline frowned back. "Don't you get pissy with me, young lady. When you're as old as I am, you use whatever advantage you can find. Something's been off, and all signs pointed to this one causing bullshit. I needed her to clearly display her deceit." She jerked a thumb toward Emma. "She just told us everything. *'Defend your property. Power takes over. Keep the upper hand.'* Fah. Those aren't our mottos. Those are a twisted, selfish variation, and now I know why the Wilson pack has failed over the past years. She's been poisoning us from within."

Emma glared at her aunt. "Defend your pack. Love over power. Keep the upper path. Those words are nothing. They mean nothing."

"They mean something when you live them," Ermeline snapped.

As the women continued to argue, Jace, Del, and Lance slipped into position in case Ermeline needed help. It was clear who the true troublemaker was.

While Ermeline wasn't Jasper pack, she wasn't in the wrong.

Something is about to happen, FB warned Blue. *Not bad but tangled.*

Damn it. That's a shitty warning, Blue complained.

Watch Steph. She's... FB paused. *Oh. One minute. This might hurt, but I'll be back. I promise.*

FB's voice faded.

A second later, Blue gasped as something inside him twisted. A sharp pain, somewhere between shifting and being impaled on a stake.

"Blue?" Stephanie ignored the other drama entirely, and she was there, supporting him as he wavered on his feet.

Holy shit. He felt torn in two, and his wolf... "What was that?"

Steph frowned. "What did you—"

A second earthquake hit, harder than the first one. This time it truly was Stephanie who kept him standing, or he would have become a Blue puddle on the ground. His limbs ached, and his vision was a little out of focus, as if he were seeing the world from two slightly different viewpoints.

You're okay. I'm back, FB told him. *Sorry about that, but now Stephanie knows.*

Knows what? And what the hell did you do?

Later. It's time...

19

———

Stephanie had spent the past hour in a semi-blur. The only thing that made sense was to keep doing the next thing.

Chased by a bat-wielding wild woman? Okay. Have a gun pointed at her by the mirror image of a past nightmare? Yeah, she could have skipped that one, but she thought she'd handled it well.

But talking sense into Dwight, explaining what Marvin and the rest of them were, plus finding out Emma expected someone to die?

The only current thought bouncing in Steph's brain was that the blood-thirsty woman really needed therapy, and she needed it now.

I can fix this.

Again, not FB. Just Stephanie having a *Me, Myself, and I* moment where the right path forward wasn't a path at all. It was like seeing the escape route went out the window of a twelve-story building, and she was about to jump out anyway because—

Because it was the right thing to do.

So much of what had gone wrong ever since they got to Jasper was on Emma's tab. Stephanie knew it. Knew it to her core.

What's more, she could *see* it...

As if she'd been dropped onto a theater seat, Stephanie watched Emma approach an older woman rocking slowly on the porch of Timberwolf Lodge. The building was the falling down mess that had existed in the spring.

"Auntie Rachel." Emma leaned on the railing and made a face. "You need to do some repairs soon or burn the place down."

"Repairs are a better option, I think," Auntie Rachel said. "I've lost the heart for it, though."

"You know, I love Timberwolf Lodge. Let me take over. I'll make sure it becomes something special. A solid place for a pack to grow."

A snort escaped Auntie Rachel. "Please." She eyed her niece. "Since when do you care about the lodge? I've asked you before for help, and you never had the time."

"I was helping Auntie Ermeline. Can't be in two places at the same time, you know," Emma said coyly.

"Ermeline told you to move out and grow up. Said you'd freeloaded off her for long enough." A dismayed noise escaped Emma, and Rachel pointed at her with amusement. "Don't look so shocked. We might be older, sugar, but we're smart enough to talk to each other. You're always there for the handout moments. Never there to help or support. Ermeline won't give you her home, and I see no reason to give you mine."

"No one else wants the trainwreck." Emma's voice lost the fake sweetness. "Jace is gone. Pete has his restaurant. Of all your nieces and nephews, only Blue is really in a place he could take over, and he's too busy being ooey, gooey, goody-two-shoes Omega to the pack."

"Maybe you're right." Auntie Rachel shrugged. "Which is why I set up a lottery and gave it away."

The screech from Emma echoed off the walls. The sound flipped Stephanie from scene to new scene.

Emma, snooping though Timberwolf Lodge and finding the contact information for Cassidy, Stacy, and Steph. Emma, sending the directions to Stacy that sent her and the boys into the heart of the river. Emma, dropping in at the law office to poke around and somehow sneaking a peek at the contact information for Dwight.

She'd lied and harassed innocent people. She'd dove into drugs to try to make herself stronger and faster.

Emma was the problem.

Stephanie was the solution.

Stephanie was still holding Blue. She twisted toward him. "I need to do something. You going to be okay?"

"I am now if you are. I'm yours," he reminded her.

Which meant everything. *Everything.* "I love you."

"Good." He winked. "Also, I love you, too."

When she stepped forward, he was at her side.

Stephanie cleared her throat. Somehow that's all it took for the squabbling to cease and all eyes to turn toward her.

"Cool. You do that?" she asked Blue.

"I...think so? Or we did?" The amusement in his voice was clear. "This afternoon is a kick so far. I have no idea what the next fancy Omega trick is going to be."

"No tricks," she assured him. "Only justice."

She met Cassidy's gaze with a silent request.

Cassidy nodded.

With Blue beside her, Stephanie adjusted until she was standing directly before Emma. "Enough."

Emma stopped sneering at her aunt to focus on Stephanie instead. "Did I ask for your bullshit opinion?"

"Danger at the gates, Emma," Ermeline warned. "You don't want to offend the Omega's mate."

"She's a human. What's she going to do to me? Talk me to death?"

"I don't want anyone dead," Stephanie said clearly. It was so, *so* true, and knowing that made it easier to do the right thing now. "You've caused more than enough hurt and fear to this pack. You're the one who will be moving, Emma."

Emma raised a brow. "Am I? You and what army are going to do this?"

Stephanie squeezed Blue's fingers then pointed with her free hand at Emma's heart. "No army. Just your wolf."

As if the past days of talking alone with FB had turned a key inside Steph, she connected with that part of Emma that was her wild side, and only her wild side. The wolf listened for a moment, then shivered. She went to her belly, tucked her nose under her paws, and lay still.

A bare second later, Emma clutched at her belly, gasping for air as if Stephanie had sliced her deep with a knife.

"What did you do to her?" Ermeline asked quietly when Emma finally settled into quiet sobs.

"I didn't do anything. Her wolf did." Stephanie squeezed Blue once more then let go, patting his arm gently. "My mate taught me some things recently. And the wolves of the pack. I'm not a wolf, Mrs. Wilson. Neither are my sister or my best friend, but we've always been somewhat wolf-like. We're like a pack—we love unconditionally, and we'd do anything for each other, including lay down our lives if necessary.

"We have honour. Just like real wolves."

Stephanie twisted to examine Emma, who was curled up on the ground now, her eyes wide with horror. "Except for Emma. She has no honour, and her animal is ashamed. Her wolf doesn't want to be with her right now."

"My wolf." Emma whispered the words.

"She's still there." Stephanie wouldn't lie to make this any tougher, no matter how much Emma deserved it. "If you give up control, you can still shift. She'll be fully in charge while you're a wolf. You won't be involved—you won't see, or hear, or run with her. You'll be shut out from each other until she's no longer appalled by the human she's paired with."

"If Emma learns honour, her wolf will return to normal?" Cassidy asked it quietly, the horror of the punishment drifting from the pack a tangible feeling.

"Yes." Blue stepped up and answered. "I can one hundred percent promise that, Emma."

He reached down for her hand.

She eyed his fingers before slowly accepting his help to stand.

It was a somber procession that moved from the deck to the parking lot. Emma got in the back of her aunt's car, her head lowered, arms wrapped around herself as if she might go comatose.

Ermeline paused with a hand on the driver's door. "It seems somewhat inappropriate to say thank you. Or to offer congratulations on winning your prize. So I'll pretend I didn't mention those and tell you that I'm taking Emma home with me. I hope, once the initial shock wears off, that she can start to work toward restitution. Both with the Wilson family and the Jasper pack. We won't lay a timeline on that, though."

That sense of *other* stirred inside Stephanie. "If you'd like, either Blue or I can come visit occasionally. Having an Omega around might help."

Ermeline raised a brow, but she nodded slowly, her regal mantle once more in place. "You are a worth adversary." She smiled, and her entire face changed to one of an old woman who had lived life to the fullest but was still finding things to delight in. "You're also an excellent Omega wolf. Well done, child. Well done."

The instant the car topped the hill, Stephanie turned to Blue and grabbed on as tight as possible. "We did it."

"You did it." He cupped her cheek and leaned in close. "Scary Omega human."

So many impossible things had just happened, but Stephanie didn't care. Right now, this moment, the only thing she wanted, needed, hoped for was Blue's arms around her and his lips on hers.

Claiming her. Claiming him.

So that's what she did.

BLUE THOROUGHLY ENJOYED KISSING his mate. Stuck together like two burrs—he held her, she clung to him—and they kissed. It seemed the perfect follow-up to the chaos. Not complicated, just right.

Meanwhile, the entire lodge was in motion around them.

"Set up by the firepit," Stacy ordered. "And break out the emergency rations. Everyone needs food, and we all need answers, and none of that can wait. We'll meet in ten minutes."

"I'm getting the good liquor," Del said. "I need something to take the edge off after seeing—"

"Don't talk about it yet," Jace slipped in quickly. "Everyone wants to know what the hell happened, but we'll only make Stephanie and Blue tell it one time."

"Got it."

More shuffling and scurrying, and then...quiet.

Stephanie pulled back just far enough to look into Blue's eyes. "Hey."

"Hey, yourself. Everything good?"

She considered then nodded. "I was worried about you. What happened when you nearly fell over?"

Blue turned her and tucked her under his arm, pacing together around the deck toward the gathering spot. "I think FB did a test run, just to make sure Emma's wolf could take charge."

Stephanie froze on the spot, her face the one twisted in horror now. "He cut you off? Completely?"

"Only for a few seconds." He stroked the line between her brows and tried to sooth her. "I understood after. And I did kind of have advance warning it was possible, considering all those conversations between you and FB that I wasn't a part of."

"Being left out of a conversation isn't having your wolf severed." She tugged him down until she could kiss his forehead. "I'm sorry you had to deal with that."

"Nothing to be sorry for, but if it makes it better, I forgive you for not knowing what FB would do with your question. I assume you asked him for advice?"

They were walking again, Stephanie keeping their pace inchworm slow. "I did. And while everyone wants to know what's up, I think some of it we need to keep to ourselves. Walk slower."

"Agreed."

"Also..." She eyed him out of the corner of her eye. *I have the feeling this might work. Yes?*

At the sound of Steph's voice in his head, Blue tripped over his own feet. Since she was tucked under his arm, he took her out with him, and they ended up in a pile with her sprawled on top.

Laughter rang out, and she pushed upright to stare down with dancing mischief in her eyes. *I thought you wolves were all about the talking mind-to-mind magic?*

We are—I am...

Blue's heart was about to explode with happiness.

And confusion.

How are we doing this? We're not mates yet.

She planted her fists on her hips. *Look, Mr. Omega. You're constantly breaking all the rules, yet you think our mating would follow a set path? Dreamer.*

So close to perfect. *We're mates.*

Looks that way.

He was too happy to move. Just lay there and grinned at her.

At least until a little boy face appeared over his, Ace's upside frown in place. "Mom says you guys are supposed to stop wrestling and come to the firepit. But you're not wrestling, are you?"

"Nope." Stephanie scooped him off his feet and plopped him down on Blue's chest. "But now we are."

Ace's squeals of delight echoed over the lake and back.

Blue was still grinning when the three of them joined the pack by the firepit.

Dwight had been popped into a private cabin to have a shower and a rest before they clarified what had just happened.

Explaining what had happened in the trees to the remaining pack took less time than expected. Most of it was logical, except the parts that made everyone shake their heads. Most of those involved Emma's deceit.

Stephanie rested in Blue's lap, the two of them in the starring position where everyone could see and hear them easily. "The part I don't know is who was the wolf you went tracking? The third member of Emma's team, if we go with Dwight being an unwilling partner number two."

"Carolyn. I have a feeling she also didn't know what she was getting into. I think when she figured out Emma was losing it, Carolyn took off. She went straight to the territory boundary and left."

"Poor kid." Steph made a face. "We need to talk to her. Make sure she doesn't think any of this was her fault."

"Do it on the sly." Jace tipped his chin toward Stacy. "Invite a few of the teens over for a movie night or something. Then our pack Omegas can pull a sneak attack and settle any concerns."

Cassidy folded her arms over her chest and grinned at her bestie. "Omega."

Steph stuck out her tongue.

Stacy snickered. "I could have sworn you said you were giving that up, now that you're an adult and all."

"It's not a childish move. Now it's an Omega move, and yes—I have no idea how, but I seem to have fallen into *woo-woo magical me* land."

"*And* fully mated. Which you weren't when you left here this morning." Del raised a brow. He glanced at the kids, then back at Blue and Steph. "That must have been some hike in the woods."

"Shut up," Blue offered dryly, but his amusement kept growing. "As Steph reminded me, rule breakers like to break rules. We seem to have missed the...usual requirements... and still ended up in Matesville."

"Good for you." Stacy pulled Ace's burning marshmallow out of the fire, blew it out, then popped it between crackers for him all while keeping her attention on Blue. "Welcome to the family, *brother*-in-law."

Well, damn. "Cool. Hi, sis." He flashed a thumbs-up at Del. "Bro! Now we're like cousin-brothers."

An enormous snort escaped Cassidy before she straightened her expression. "Um, no. But you are now part of a bigger family. And I'm glad."

Lance and Sophie took all four kids to an unstomped on snowy area to build miniature snowmen. Marvin was given pats on the back for his work that day. He took the thanks in stride until Del's assistant Angie marched up and planted one on him, right on the lips.

Watching the moose man blush made Blue's day even brighter.

The party was in full swing when Stephanie caught him by the hand and tugged him toward the front of the house. *Come with me.*

I adore that we can talk like this, he shared. *Where are we going?*

Secrets.

One of which was that Birdie sat parked outside the lodge.

"You got my car."

"Lance got your car." Steph slipped behind the wheel.

Blue got into the passenger seat with amusement. "Where are you taking me?"

Home.

That sense of warmth just kept rising.

She tugged him in his front door, a wicked smile

twisting her lips. "Are we okay in terms of all the magic stuff that went down today? All clear and in order?"

"No, but that's part of the joy of being an Omega. We *like* to make stuff up as we go along." Blue carefully closed and locked the door then crowded toward her. "And one of the joys of being pack is there are always people at our back. They'll tell us if there's more we need to share."

Stephanie's back hit the bedroom door. Blue placed a hand on the doorframe over her head and smoldered down at her.

She fit here so well. In his house. In his heart.

In his head. *I love you.*

I love you, too.

She ducked around him, diving for his bed. A second later—damn, she was nearly as good as a wolf at stripping—they were both naked and she was in his lap. A wonderfully erotic position, all things considered.

Stephanie kissed her way along his jaw. *Nice part about talking like this is I can kiss you at the same time.*

Don't break anything multi-tasking, he teased. *I like you in one piece.*

I like you in pieces. She nipped his earlobe and every nerve in his body charged to one hundred and ten percent. It was his every hot and dirty erotic dream button.

Blue grabbed on tight. He didn't want to react by tossing her to the mattress and fucking her into tomorrow.

Steph slid her wet core over his cock, and it was the next thing to paradise. She levered up, slid down. Even better.

He was trying to keep his head on straight when she bit him again.

Slow and controlled went out the window. Thankfully, Stephanie was as frantic for him as he was for her, and between the two of them, his bed was shaking in seconds flat. The sound of his panting excitement, the sound of pleasure on her lips.

"Steph." Blue adjusted position just enough to rub hard on her clit.

She broke. "Yes."

He went over the next wave with her, both laughing and hugging each other, a multitude of kisses dancing between them.

It was a long time before she pulled back and smoldered at him. "Hey, mate."

"Hey."

Steph rolled, tucking herself into his arms, right where she belonged. "We're on our honeymoon."

"Are we?"

"Yes. Because we have a pack who can take care of things without us for a few days. And we have a family who know when to be supportive and let people celebrate a good thing in their lives."

And you are mates. Which means you should spend time together to strengthen your bond. Although I think it's strong already.

Steph's eyes widened. "Did you hear that?"

Thank God. "That was FB, wasn't it?"

She nodded. "Good. I wondered what would happen with that."

I can still talk only to Stephanie if I want, but I don't think that's necessary very often.

"Just when we want to plan a surprise birthday party, or something, yes?" Steph asked.

Silly humans.

FB went silent, so Blue went back to focusing on the most important person in the room. "Are you happy, love?"

She considered then nodded. "I am. Not because my

family is, although I'm glad they are. Not because we won Timberwolf Lodge, although I'm glad we did. I'm happy because I have you."

Perfect. "Me too. Getting to have you. Friend. Lover. Mate."

The most perfect prize for any Omega.

20

———

inter had truly arrived, painting Timberwolf
Lodge with a Christmas card layer of white.
The sunlight sparkled off the glistening layers, and
everywhere Blue looked, signs of the holiday season were
mixed with the proof happy wolves and children lived here.

The toboggan hill had been packed down to the point
that a good glide would carry a wolf nearly to the middle of
the frozen lake, on their belly or on a sled.

The pack was growing. Dwight had decided to stay in
town, and he and one of Angie's friends had begun dating.
Marvin was full-on wooing Angie. The last time Stephanie
had seen the moose he'd been talking to himself, debating
poetry or flowers as the next best gift to take her.

Stacy sighed happily. "Look at them. I mean, just
look at them." She gestured at her boys, who were in the
midst of the pack children, happy as pigs in mud. Ace
and Blaze raced around with arms outspread like they
were airplanes. Colt was in his wolf form, head down,
tail up, barking enthusiastically like a puppy before
pouncing on his new best friend. The two of them

rolled down the toboggan hill, excitement echoing off the mountains when they finally got their paws under them.

"Yeah, I guess they're pretty cute." Cassidy sipped her tea with an exaggerated nonchalance. "Guess it's a good thing. Jace and I have ordered one for delivery in the spring."

It took a second, then Stephanie and her sister were both up, squealing with delight as they squeezed Cassidy and offered her congratulations. It took a few minutes before they settled back down to finish their visit.

"It seemed like an okay time to start a family, considering how well everything's going in the pack."

"Del says a lot of the new growth is because the pack finally has a full leadership team." Stacy leaned forward and whispered softly. "I think it's because the three of us kick ass and take names."

Stephanie stretched her feet out and rested them on her sister's knee. "This is what you get when you put your mind to it. Set a few intentions and take a chance."

"That's another thing I find really amusing. The fact that you've always talked like that, the *listen to the universe* mumbo jumbo, but now everybody hears it and goes, 'Ooh, the Omega has spoken.' As if you didn't just mutter whatever the hell words popped into your head, but somehow the gobbledygook makes people happy."

Stephanie pressed her fingers gently to her chest and spoke as if she were high royalty. "If it is our duty to amuse the masses, then we shall do our utmost." She wrapped an arm around Cassidy's shoulders, pressing a kiss to her cheek. "Also, it makes me happy. I figure Omega is as good a job description as any."

"To having the right jobs for the right person, in the

right place." Stacy lifted her mug in the air. "Hip, hip, hooray."

"Higgity piggity." Stephanie snorted. "Sorry, not a word."

"It works." Cassidy finished the ritual. "Huggity. I love you guys."

"Love you, too," echoed all around.

Cassidy looked thoughtful. "It's not just the jobs we get to do or that we look forward to having Timberwolf Lodge full of guests. We have three great guys. And we're all head over heels in love."

"Who knew that was going to happen when you tossed our names into the hat for Timberwolf Lodge?" Stacy agreed.

No, Stephanie thought. None of them had known what they were going to find when they came out on the adventure.

But maybe that was part of the reward—taking those first steps and following them through to the end. Somewhere along the way, good things were going to happen.

Her friends left to join the pack building snow forts by the lakeshore. Stephanie had spotted Blue walking toward her, so she rearranged the cushions and the blankets and patted the spot next to her for him to cuddle in on the bench so they could look out over the wintry scene.

Hello, my love.

Hello to you, too.

He kissed her, sweet and hot, his hands drifting under the blanket to interesting places. When he stopped, she was very warm indeed. "Nice of you to drop in. Tell me we're going somewhere private very soon."

"Soon. But for now, I was doing some math."

Stephanie raised a brow. "Do I need to break out my notebook?"

He laughed. "It's just that I was feeling sorry for myself earlier this year. Jace and Cassidy became mates right away after arriving here. Then Stacy showed up, and she and Del ended up mates, bada-boom, bada-bing."

"Very musical math."

He caught her by the hand. "Did you know that you and I set the record?"

"I'm pretty sure Lance and Sophie did that with their *sexy eyes touching sexy eyes and poof, we're mates* insta-love."

Blue waved his hand. "I mean out of everybody who did things without the insta-love trick."

Stephanie curled up beside him, arms resting around his shoulders. "Tell me. You're obviously dying to."

"Please. I think we decided there was going to be no dying or death threats allowed anywhere around Timberwolf Lodge for the next year. At least."

She snickered.

"So, the math says that from the moment Jace told me Cassidy was his mate to that becoming true, twenty-five days passed."

"Slacker."

"You are so perfect for me. Now Del. We'll give him a bit of the benefit of the doubt. Because he started sniffing around Timberwolf Lodge before Stacy even arrived."

Stephanie wrinkled her nose. "Ugh. I had forgotten about that. He's my brother-in-law. I don't want to remember him sniffing around me."

"Wolves sniff, it's a fact of life. There are some burdens we have to bear." He lifted his fingers and dropped the five to a four. "Twenty-four days."

"Get out. That's funny."

Blue tapped on Stephanie's nose. "But you and me? We are a magical miracle."

"You must be using that new math or something because you knew I was your mate the same moment Jace laid eyes on Cassidy. Or that's the story I heard."

Blue shook his head. "I knew you were the *possibility* of being my mate, which was gosh-darn confusing, to be honest. The first moment that I knew for certain you were *going* to be my mate was when we got stuck up at the cabin."

Oh really? "Now that you say that, I remember thinking the day before the cabin that I liked you. As in, I *liked* liked you."

"Which means between then and officially becoming mates was exactly ten days. Ta-da."

She pressed her fingers to her mouth to cover her smirk. "It's not always a contest, but go us."

Blue tucked his arm around her, and they sat quietly and stared out over their pack. Laughter swelled from the children. One of the teens started singing a sea shanty, and soon the lot of them were at it, those in wolf form howling at the appropriate moments.

Jace offered a wave then picked Cassidy up and headed for the trees, his mate laughing so hard Stephanie heard it in her heart.

Del and Stacy had just loaded their entire family onto a long sled, swooshing down the hill at high speed. They hit a bump and all five of them went in different directions. Somehow Del caught Ace and slid under Stacy before they hit the ground, the group of them ending up in a puppy pile of happiness and belonging.

"I like being here," Stephanie admitted. "It really feels like home."

"It's just a place," Blue said softly. "It's the people who make it more."

He lifted her hand to his lips and kissed it. His eyes sharp on her, full of so much love.

He was right, of course. Not the pretty building or the gorgeous mountains. It was them, all of them. Right where they were supposed to be.

Home at Timberwolf Lodge.

~

New York Times Bestselling Author Vivian Arend
brings you a light-hearted paranormal trilogy
Timberwolf Lodge.

WIN A WILDERNESS LODGE!

Ready for the chance of a lifetime? Enter now to become
the new owners of the Timberwolf Lodge located near
Jasper, Alberta. You'll have one year to meet the set
conditions and the lodge will be all yours!

Small print: (very, very, very small print)
Warning: Lodge may contain werewolves, fated mates, and
tons of shifter pack drama.
Good luck, and have fun! Don't die!

~

Timberwolf Lodge
The Alpha Option
The Enforcer's Gamble
The Omega's Prize

~

ABOUT THE AUTHOR

New York Times and *USA Today* bestselling author Vivian Arend loves to share the products of her over-active imagination with her readers. She writes contemporary, western, and light-hearted paranormal romances. The stories are humorous yet emotional, usually with a large cast of family or friends, and a guaranteed happily-ever-after. Vivian lives in British Columbia, Canada, with her husband of many years—her inspiration for every hero and a willing companion for all sorts of adventures.

www.vivianarend.com